SOUTH OF FIFTY-THREE

Blood Ritual:
The Adventures of Scarlet and Bradshaw, Volume 1
BY THEODORE ROSCOE

Champion of Lost Causes
BY MAX BRAND

The City of Stolen Lives: The Adventures
of Peter the Brazen, Volume 1
BY LORING BRENT

The Complete Cabalistic Cases of Semi Dual,
the Occult Detector, Volume 2: 1912–13
BY J.U. GIESY AND JUNIUS B. SMITH

Doan and Carstairs: Their Complete Cases
BY NORBERT DAVIS

The King Who Came Back
BY FRED MacISAAC

The Radio Gun-Runners
BY RALPH MILNE FARLEY

The Scarlet Blade: The Rakehelly Adventures of
Cleve and d'Entreville, Volume 1
BY MURRAY R. MONTGOMERY

Sabotage
BY CLEVE F. ADAMS

SOUTH OF FIFTY-THREE

JACK BECHDOLT

ALTUS PRESS
2016

© 2016 Steeger Properties, LLC, under license to Altus Press • First Edition—2016

EDITED AND DESIGNED BY
Matthew Moring

PUBLISHING HISTORY
"South of Fifty-Three" originally appeared in the March 25 and April 1, 8, 15, 22,
    and 29, 1922 issues of *Argosy All-Story Weekly* magazine (Vol. 141, No. 4–Vol.
    142, No. 3). Copyright © 1922 by The Frank A. Munsey Company.

THANKS TO
Gary A. Buckingham

ISBN
978-1-61827-234-8

Visit *altuspress.com* for more books like this.
Printed in the United States of America.

TABLE OF CONTENTS

CHAPTER I

FANGS OF THE SEA

THERE WAS ONE cigarette left in her smart silver case, and Marion Reade judged that this was the minute to light it. By the time the cigarette had burned out the uncertainty of the last few hours would be certainty. The big question would be answered—perhaps all questions would be answered for all time. The fleet gray waves ran swiftly like the hunting wolf pack; here and there one showed white fangs. Sometimes one slapped the flank of the launch wallowing disabled, and sent in a small flood to swell the oily, dirty accumulation slopping in the bilge, much as though some wolf bolder and more impatient than its fellows had reached in its paw to seize her.

For hours the shouldering gray wolves of the sea had been running like this, hurrying up out of the black fog of the narrowed horizon, showing their white fangs at the drifting launch and speeding past. Now the craft had drifted close enough to reveal the gaunt, gray reef that was their rendezvous.

Wind and tide were setting the launch onto the reef, and the girl knew that nothing could be done about it. More or less consciously she had saved that last cigarette for this moment before the launch struck the reefs. It suited her sense of the dramatic to await the issue this way. It seemed a fitting expression of a very modern young woman's proper attitude toward the three very old, blind, blundering, and rather ridiculous legendary females who are supposed to weave the threads of human lives—and make a jolly fine mess of the job!

1

With all the peculiar advantages of 1921 and the sureness of twenty-two years, Marion Reade never doubted that she could have filled the roles of all three Fates, using modern business efficiency and business methods to accomplish the intricate tasks they muddled through. Being denied that privilege, she could only express her utter contempt of their management of the cosmos. The cigarette epitomized it. It does not follow that she was particularly fond of tobacco. All the women she knew smoked. It was the thing. The lady's pipe, and cigar, those exotic importations from England, really were much the newer methods, but the cigarette was enough for Marion.

She often wondered, in private, if the habit was worth the trouble. Sometimes the smoke hurt her eyes and gave her a sore throat. She set the last cigarette in her amber and platinum holder, lighted it, cocked her boots impudently on the coaming of the boat, and blew out a cloud of smoke with the gesture of supreme contempt.

If Death really were waiting for her over there on that reef where the slaty waves boomed; if this were the end of twenty-two years of life that had not been half bad when one considered—and the end of all the plans and aspirations of a crowded future which was very dear to her—if Death really awaited her there, she was game to look him in the eye and grin and hail him with the current phrase of good fellowship: "Hello, Old-Timer!"

The girl drifting in a groggy launch, its engine disabled, at the mercy of the merciless North Pacific and the gaunt, gray-fanged reef of some Alaskan island not even worthy a name, in all outward appearance was as foreign to the drear picture as a peacock among vultures. Her dress was the dress of vanity—the theatrical tailor's idea of apparel suitable for a lady explorer. It would have done well for a girl-and-music show—or the runway of the Follies. From the trim brown boots, still showing signs of recent varnishings, to the sports hat with a foolish feather, her one idea was to charm the masculine eye, particularly the city-bred eye that would see nothing ridiculous in these neatly fitting knickers, the jauntiness of the belted tweed shooting-coat, the silk shirt with its soft collar fastened by a gold bar pin when worn in that grim outpost of the last frontier, Alaska.

She was a slight woman, not above five and a half feet in height. Her figure was boyish, and there was something boyish too in the straightforward look of the brown eyes, blinking a little now at the annoyance of cigarette smoke. Her hair had been bobbed. It was the old-gold hue of weathered straw, and curled in spite of the fog. She had been adrift in the launch more than eight hours, and yet in all the damp and discomfort and peril had kept some of that spruceness, that precocity, that overemphasis of utter inutility which was the hall-mark of her own proper background and environment—Broadway. A bit of the true Broadway—street of electric signs, tinsel, and tawdry—she drifted in a bleak, wild sea like a fluff of thistle-down, cocking her foolish boots on the boat's coaming, smoking a cigarette in an amber holder, a vanity case open on her knee while she powdered her nose in readiness to charm one more male—this time one of royal blood and undisputed sway—King Death.

Eight hours ago that easily seemed eight ages the incident had begun very naturally and casually. When she remembered its beginning the present seemed fantastic beyond belief. The yacht *Frivolity* lay at anchor off a small island of the Alaskan peninsula. The brief arctic night had passed, and the sun, almost the midnight sun Marion had once read about, was high in the sky and gleaming pale through thickening fog banks.

Douglas Fox, owner of the yacht, whose guest she was on this two months' midsummer cruise of Alaska waters, had a burning ambition to slaughter a Kodiak bear. Irving Beach, also a guest—the Irving Beach, of New York, big-game hunter, and himself the coveted prize of many a feminine hunter of big matrimonial game on Manhattan—already had killed a bear and a moose in their sport along the Alaskan peninsula, and was generously ready to further his host's ambition. They had gone ashore to try their luck on the island; Marion Reade went with them, avid for new thrills and shrewdly aware of the sensational story this would make to carry home. Nor was she totally unaware that she had been growing in the estimation of Irving Beach—a state of affairs well worth the consideration of so shrewd a girl. Once ashore, Marion Reade discovered that big-game hunting consisted of something more than planting a deadly bullet square in the spinal cord of an animated bear rug—and leaving the details to a taxidermist. On this lonely island of a wilderness coast it consisted largely in breaking a trail over the roughest kind of country, fighting through tangling brier thickets, scaling steep rocks, clambering over and crawling under windfalls, up and down, in mud and mire, with every leafy branch shedding a douche of icy water at the touch, the chill, fog-wreathed wind pinching exposed flesh, and mosquitoes everywhere—mosquitoes capable of driving even an Indian mad.

Marion stuck it out two hours, then left the party. That was mere common sense and fair sportsmanship. She was an encumbrance, and she knew it. Besides, there was no fun in it for her—and she very well understood that the constant drenching, the mud, the briers, and the swelling lumps of many mosquito bites were not enhancing her beauty in the eyes of Irving Beach.

Refusing all offers of escort, she went back to the cove where the launch waited. The sailor assigned to it had wandered away on business of his own. Marion had handled the launch before, and disdained waiting for him. More than anything else she wanted, just then, the comfort of her own stateroom on the *Frivolity*, a bath, a change to something loose and comfortable, and the easy, good-natured companionship of Ada Fox, satisfied to rough it through Alaska with the companionship of a whole library of novels of passion, cigarettes, and boxes of candy, specially packed by the clever New York maker to keep fresh for the voyage.

Marion started bravely from the cove where the launch had landed, heedless that fog already had shut her out of sight of the yacht. To find the *Frivolity* seemed a simple matter to Marion Reade, with her complete self-assurance of youth and her modem woman's ideas of an exalted place in the scheme of things. In the fog she had played hide and seek with the *Frivolity*, but not until a playful wave had caught her hand off the steering wheel and slopped into the cockpit, drowning the gas engine, did the matter look serious. It had continued serious and more serious until this moment, most serious of all. The cigarette burned to the end, and she was almost glad, though its snuffing out signaled her own peril. She rose and looked critically at the rocks close by.

It was more than an isolated reef, she discovered now that the launch was nearer. The haze showed dimly low cliffs behind the tangle of broken boulders, streaming kelp, and white water. The swell was heavy enough to make a miniature maelstrom of the place. The rollers exploded with the roar of big guns, and the aerated water formed lesser waves that swept beyond the first line to break again and still again and rush streaming in treacherous backwash and intertwining currents.

There was no spare oar in the launch, nothing to propel or guide the useless craft. The boat's utter destruction was certain, and her own scarcely more problematical. There was a cork lifebelt, and she buckled it securely about her, grumbling even as she did: "The darn thing gives me streamlines like a washtub."

Then there was no more to do than pick her moment before the boat crashed and go over the side in the hope of winning through. What she might win to, drowning in the surf or a more lingering death by starvation on some desolate rock forgotten in a forgotten part of the world, she avoided considering. The slim chance of living was offered; she had profited often by taking slim chances. The color ebbed from her cheeks, leaving exposed glaring patches that were artifice. The brown eyes blinked for a moment to shut out the picture.

Through lips that were white and in a voice not so sure as she would have it the girl expressed her opinion to beguile the waiting: "I'd give a lot to have Annette Kellerman double for me right now." The helpless launch rose high on the back of a comber. Marion could feel the lift of the big wave and see it curling to crash against a spine of granite. The backwash of the wave ahead was pouring off the reef, and she had a few seconds' clear view of jagged rock laid bare, of the weeds that clung to it, even the shells of barnacles spotting it. When the launch was flung by the playful wave against that barrier it would cease to be a launch speedily.

A few seconds ahead of the crash she was over the side, trusted to the onrushing roller, but with hope renewed. Her last brief look at the universe before that plunge discovered the silhouette of a man against the foggy sky—a man staring intently at her from the summit of one of the low cliffs. Even as she dived she was conscious that the man had waved an arm excitedly, a token that she had been seen by him. If she could last through the next ten minutes' struggle all would be well. If! She chose her wave wisely. It carried her far before it broke, far enough to gain the top of a rock, larger, flatter, and higher than the rest.

The backwash flooded knee deep about her. Her feet slipped on the weedy surface, and she went down in the current that streamed toward the sea. Still she managed to cling with one hand to a projection, though her arm ached with the strain of it. Nose and mouth were full of stinging salt water. She choked and struggled and was conscious of the bitter cold that soon ends the efforts of the strongest swimmers in this part of the world.

Marion Reade was not strong, nor particularly skillful. A little play in the tame surf of Long Beach and Atlantic City— that, and a great deal of parade on the sands—was her equipment for this struggle. There was a pause then, when the flood had ebbed and the rock lay bare. She scrambled to her feet and shouted her loudest. She saw again a man's silhouette, then two of them, on the cliff top. She saw something else happen, fantastic, weird, terrible.

One of the misty figures performed a swift pantomime of a

man raising and sighting a rifle. The rifle was aimed at her. She heard no report, but the unmistakable snarling whine of a bullet close by her head told her he had fired. The performance so astounded and outraged her that Marion remained exactly as she was, upright and staring at her would-be murderer, making an excellent target. Another bullet spoke from the fog, a waspish, ill-natured warning. She flung herself face down on the rock and clung there.

Deliberately more shots followed.

Whoever was on the cliff was making a conscientious effort to kill her. She was not afraid nor conscious of the cold nor the imminent probability of drowning or being dashed to death among the rocks; she burned with indignation against the in-comprehensible inhumanity that inhabited this strange island and welcomed the shipwrecked waif with bullets. Had there been any way to do it, she was in the frame of mind to march deliberately into the murderer's fire and, if she lived through, kill him with her bare hands.

Another wave drenched her, and she began the old fight to hold the rock with all the strength and cunning and courage she could summon—just as if to hold the rock meant safety and not eventual annihilation by rifle fire!

When she breathed again she was conscious that more than one marksman was sending his lead after her. The rock had become the target of a hailstorm of bullets. She could hear the faint popping of rifles and shouting of men. It was not a moment to guess what motive was behind all this weird murderousness; it was not a time to spend in consideration of any sort. The rock was no longer tenable if she wanted to live. And she was angry enough now, by some strange alchemy of jangled emotions, to live in spite of machine-gun fire.

She could not go back to the sea. The shore was the only refuge, if that could be considered refuge. She slipped off the rock, head first, like a seal, and the boiling white current flung her violently toward the land, bruising her, beating out her breath, clutching her fast.

Several times her feet found the sand only to lose it again. She floundered among the rocks, more weakly, without conscious plan, instinct driving her on. She was conscious of renewed shooting, shouts, and the sudden apparition of a huge figure of a man materialized from the mist that splashed into the surf and came floundering toward her. She ceased to care much if he reached her—nothing seemed to matter any more.

In a vague way she knew she had been caught up in the man's arms, and that they were on the sand. He was forcing her roughly behind big boulders, shouting at her to keep her head down and to follow him. As in some grotesque nightmare they crawled then, on all fours, among broken rock and tidal pools, and bullets snarled about them.

All rhyme or reason had gone out of events. Marion Reade was doing what she was told to do automatically, conscious only of a sickening fear of things she could not understand and the vague clamor of the reasoning part of her brain that this was all phantasmagoria.

She was picked up suddenly and knew she was being carried at a stumbling run, and that was the end for a time.

CHAPTER II

JONATHAN HAYES

MARION READE LAY under blankets in the best bunk the small ranch-house afforded; she had been there several hours, tended by an Aleut Indian woman, and occasionally by the white man who now sat near by, interestedly watching her. During that time she had approached conscious speech several times only to slip back over the border to the forgetfulness that was making up for her long exposure and suffering at sea.

The girl looked very small under blankets. Her short, curling hair spread out fanwise about her face, and made the features seem even more delicate and somewhat uncanny in their beauty. A bare arm lay exposed; her hand groped restlessly, searching.

Several times the watcher had been startled by her opening eyes, the quickening of intelligence in her expression, and her sudden starting up. So far she had not spoken. Shock perhaps had stopped her tongue, or weariness. But at each partial wakening began the puzzling pantomime of a search for something she seemed to miss.

Her hosts were mystified and curious. The man who watched Marion was a big fellow in height and girth, splendidly proportioned. His shoulders were broad and heavily muscled. He was smooth shaven. Hair and eyes were dark, and the face was grave. He looked like a man of determination and will power, but the arched eyebrows and the dark eyes that widened readily at every move of the restless patient suggested imagination, quick intelligence, perhaps idealism. He was dressed comfortably for the country he lived in, wearing a heavy wool shirt that hung unbelted and outside the trousers like a Russian smock over a close fitting, faded jersey. The trouser legs had been stuffed into native mukluks of seal hide, waterproof, light and warm.

Leaning forward, he gave earnest, eager attention to the woman the sea had brought him. He sat with hands on knees; a rifle was conveniently near his chair. In that house of squared logs chinked with moss, simple but comfortable, he seemed rightly placed as an unusually fine specimen of his race.

Without warning the girl sat up in bed and drew the blankets about her shoulders. The lovely bare arm and finely shaped hand that terminated it began to search among the folds like something endowed with a separate intelligence.

The man rose hastily and came close to the bunk.

From a near-by shelf he took the various articles of Marion Reade's amusing wardrobe, dried and cleaned and ready for her use. He began again a pantomime repeated several times, offering them in the hope of satisfying whatever want she felt. One by one the items were rejected—knickers, silk shirt, coat, the cigarette case. There remained the little jeweled vanity case. That was what she sought! Her hand snatched it up and snapped open its cover.

The patient looked critically at her reflection in the tiny mirror, turning and twisting her head about and frowning at what she saw. Her deft fingers began to work with practiced speed, using powder puff and rouge and the little pencils of cosmetics.

The whole-hearted astonishment of the man passed her by. She had more pressing business to dispose of first. He could wait. When the task was done she turned her brown eyes his way and smiled, asking his approval in dumb show.

Up to that moment she acted automatically, according to firmly fixed habit, without memory of the past or consciousness of the present.

Then she became aware of the blankets that swathed her; of

the man who gaped at her as if she were some curious thing dredged out of the sea or fallen from another planet; of the low-roofed room, unceiled, and the fire glowing on a big, rude hearth which gave them their only light; of the Indian woman kneeling there, busy with an iron kettle; of the windows shuttered by thick, rude planks; of the strange, quiet, strained atmosphere of the place, with its simple furniture and primitive people.

Marion exclaimed, bewildered: "What's this? Where's Douglas—Ada—Beach—everybody?"

The man answered soothingly: "You're all right. Among friends—safe."

The peculiar resonance of that voice roused her strained nerves to unreasoning anger. She remembered then, and memory of her landing gave her anger reasonable excuse.

She said with bitterness: "Safe! So that's your idea of humor!"

He repeated patiently, mildly: "We don't mean you any harm."

She noticed, with the vividness of first impressions, that his speech was slow, a little deliberate, as if his English, perfect as it was, was unfamiliar to his tongue. Her antagonism puzzled her, but just the sound of his voice seemed to lash her to anger. "I don't know where this is—or who 'we' are, but—"

"This is Kalvik Island."

"Then all I have to say is that you Kalvik Islanders have a rare idea of hospitality. Do you always try to murder shipwrecked strangers—women especially? It seems such a waste of bullets. Why not let them drown?"

The big man's face flushed painfully. He leaned forward, very much in earnest. "Those were Cook's men!" he exclaimed. "Please believe we wouldn't do a thing like that!"

"I don't know whose men—"

"No—I suppose not. But bad as they are, I don't think they would have fired if they had known you were a woman. Even I didn't know that until I carried you to the house. Probably they thought it was a rescue of some sort—somebody come to help me." He saw her bewilderment, and explained hurriedly: "I said you were safe here. You are if I can keep you safe. But this house is in danger of Cook. We are all in danger. You see, I'm in a state of siege."

"Siege! You mean—somebody is—attacking you?"

He smiled grimly. "Yes—just that. I'm afraid you landed at a bad time—a rather awkward time. I hope you won't be sorry for it—or hold it against us." Marion's eyes were open at their widest. She sat bolt upright. "Then I'm not safe. Nobody's safe. It's a fight, and anybody's likely to get hurt—killed even!"

"I am very sorry, Miss—"

"I am Marion Reade, of New York City."

He bowed slightly. "I am Jonathan Hayes, of Kalvik Island, and very, very sorry things happened this way."

"Well," said Marion briskly, more normal now, "I can't blame you, can I? After all, I came uninvited. I seem to have dropped into a lively party."

"Party's a queer word for it!" Hayes exclaimed seriously. "There are eight men out there watching this place, planning to rush it around midnight, when it gets dark. It's only fair to tell you they're a very bad lot. They're here to murder me, and that's the size of it. But there are four of us—six, counting you and Anna, the Aleut there. And they won't harm a hair of your head as long as I am alive."

Marion's hand extended suddenly. "You said something then! And—thanks for fishing me out of the surf. Thanks awfully!"

"But how did you get there? If there's a ship near—"

"It isn't. God knows where the yacht is! Trying to find me, I suppose."

Hayes looked thoughtful. He sighed. "That's awkward. I had hoped, when I saw you, it might be a ship."

She outlined briefly her adventures with the launch. "You see they have no idea where I am—or what happened to me. They would not miss me until the men come aboard tonight.

Then—oh, they'll look, of course, but—" She shuddered. "This country—this terrible country! The miles and miles of it, bays and inlets and rivers and whole mountain ranges, whole nations and continents of it! I wish—I almost wish I had drowned!"

The man's eyes flashed. "You dare to say a thing like that—after what you've come through! No man—or woman—has the right to say such a thing. That is God's province!"

"Oh," said Marion dryly, "I didn't know I'd dropped in to church."

"Your talk is childish," Hayes answered sternly. For the moment the rebuke left her speechless. He rose. "I'll tell one of my Aleut boys to build a beacon fire. It's possible your friends might see it and come here. While I'm gone, if you feel strong enough, I'd advise you to dress. The woman will help you."

He spoke some directions to the Aleut squaw in her own tongue, and went out of the room.

Marion gasped. "Well! I started something then. And what I'd like to know is how that big hick got the notion he could give orders to me!"

The woman, Anna, came to help her dress. Marion asked her many questions about Jonathan Hayes, but Anna only shook her head and looked stupid.

"Him boss here," she muttered in a tone that seemed to settle it.

On her feet again, Marion found herself stiff and bruised. She was glad to sit down in a deep chair lined with soft pelts.

She still felt bitter resentment toward the big fellow who dared give her orders.

She sniffed derisively. "All this stuff about a state of siege! What kind of a scenario is that? I never even saw the man in my life—and I don't have to believe him. I don't believe him. I'll find out for myself."

She stood up, but found herself shaky. The room had an uncomfortable way of heaving like a ship in a storm. The walls bulged forth at her, and the floor rose and sank unexpectedly.

She sat down hurriedly and leaned back against the pile of velvety skins. She noted they were extraordinarily rich and warm. Suddenly thrilled, she knew that they were sealskins. The real thing—not the Broadway kind. Sealskins! Enough of them cushioning this chair to pay a millionaire's alimony!

Marion Reade forgot she was tired and weak. She sprang to her feet and wrapped a pelt about her shoulders, delighted with the silky touch of the fur against her cheek. She added another pelt, contriving a very fair imitation of a cape, then examined herself in a small mirror. Hugging the skins close about her, she took a turn around the room. Her childish delight in the pretties swept from memory the room, the island, the man, and the danger she had been warned against.

She imagined bright lights and people; heard the scuffling of crowds that packed broad pavements, the murmur of many yokes, honking of motor horns, clang of surface car gongs; she felt the electric thrill of Broadway as she stepped in imagination from a big, closed car and passed haughtily into a brilliant restaurant.

The Aleut woman turned from her task at the fire to watch this madness with open mouth. Hayes came, and his astonishment was as ludicrous, but it turned quickly to more personal admiration. He exclaimed, with startling evidence of conviction: "That's beautiful! You're lovely!"

Marion laughed, a light, chiming laugh, like some dainty music box. She bowed her small body mockingly and flashed a glance up at him. "Thank you kindly—for your good opinion."

"I never thought those skins could look like that. They've been waiting for years—for you to bring their beauty to life."

"They're gorgeous, Mr. Hayes—absolutely splendiferous. The darlings!"

"You like them?"

"*Like* them! Does a woman like sealskins? I'd like to see one who wouldn't pawn her immortal soul for the sweeties!" Hayes's face changed; he frowned; he said gloomily: "Women! Women like you! That's what's at the bottom of all this—your vanity and greed. It's your kind, outside there in the big cities, that incited all the robbery and murder and beastliness that wins skins like that. Every one of them stands for cruelty, often violence, often human lives. They're reeking with blood—but you wind them round your shoulders and smile. Put those skins down!"

Marion flung the skins back on the chair and faced him, tense with defiance. "When you talk to me after this you can confine your remarks to yes and no. You're a filthy beast!"

"I'm not a beast!" It was surprising to note how her words had hurt him. "I'm a decent man—and try to be a gentleman. But I've been fighting for my life, and my home, all day. And have to keep on—without much hope! Can't you forgive what a man's jumping nerves make him say? Can anything make you understand what I'm going through—with eight men against me out there?"

Marion smiled wisely. "Oh, yes—the fight! I'd forgot I'd dropped in on your private war."

"You don't believe me?"

"Well, of course, I have only your word—"

Jonathan Hayes looked white and dangerous. "Come here," he said, moving toward one of the shuttered windows. "Stand here against the wall, close. Now, watch." Keeping his body to one side of the window, he reached forward, lifted the bar from the heavy shutter, and let the thick panel swing open a few inches. Quickly he got his arm away from the window, holding the shutter at the end of the wooden bar.

They waited something less than a minute. Marion heard no shot, but the glass dial of an old-fashioned octagonal clock on the wall facing the window shattered into bits and fell tinkling. The clock's white enameled face showed a ragged, black hole exactly as if it had been the chalked target of a shooting gallery.

Jonathan Hayes closed the shutter with a bang and slipped

back the bar deftly. Two thuds told of other bullets embedded in the thick planks.

"That's what happens if you show a light," he said grimly. "Do you want more proof?"

From close by the house came an answering rattle of rifle fire.

"My Aleut boys," Hayes explained. "They won't sleep on the job."

Marion had gone white and strangely silent. If the thing still seemed fantastic beyond belief, there was the broken glass and the black hole in its dial to testify that what Hayes said was true.

She walked unsteadily toward the table and leaned against it. "Owe you—an apology—I guess. Excuse it—my own—frazzled nerves."

Hayes said eagerly: "It's all right. You owe me nothing—but you must believe what I say. And you must take orders, too. It might mean life or death, just now. Why—you're shaking! Sit down. I frightened you—like a fool!"

Marion sat down weakly. She bowed her head in her hands, which were gripped tightly. She fought to keep her teeth from chattering. But presently she looked up defiantly. "I'm not scared of any roughneck with a rifle—nor of you either! You'd better believe me—"

"There," he said kindly, "I do. Here, Anna! Food."

He pulled a chair beside hers. "Drink this hot tea. Eat some soup. You'll need it. Take it, I say."

He held the tall glass of tea, quaint relic of the Russian habit lingering among the Aleuts, to her lips. His left hand steadied her shoulders. She obeyed orders and sipped.

When she was eating the rich soup and finding it delicious in spite of the queer place and the dangers that threatened, Hayes began to speak.

"What I said about women and vanity and crime you mustn't take personally. I don't judge individuals. I don't know that I'm fit to judge your civilization, I who—" He checked this thought and frowned. "But somebody is to blame for all the wanton cruelty that robbed Alaska of the seal herds. Somebody is to blame for the crime and violence and filth that are spread by the men who serve the desires of you people outside there—desires of you women that I can only understand as vanity. If I'm wrong, excuse the ignorance of a man who doesn't know what he's talking about—who never even saw the civilization he condemns. If I'm rude, excuse that in a man who's wondering just how much longer he has to live; whose life is threatened by that same greed that serves your vanity."

"What do you mean by that?"

He answered grimly: "I mean sealskins. Those same pretty pelts you've been admiring. That's at the bottom of all this. Greed for them brought Cook here, invading my islands, shooting at every light that shows. I haven't any foolish hopes. This man Cook is here to find out what I know and won't tell him. He's tried to buy or trick me into a partnership and failed. He has come now to take the secret away from me. I dare say that nice, refined torture is his plan—if he can get hold of me. Well, it's his life or mine."

"You have sealskins hidden here?"

"Not here. But I know where they are, enough sealskins to make me a millionaire. Rather than let Cook or any man get those skins I'll let them kill me. Much good it'll do them dead!" He glowered defiantly toward the shuttered windows, evidently thinking of the riflemen who watched it.

Marion Reade puzzled over what he had said and the danger they faced. She was faintly consoling with her: "Perhaps the yacht will come! If it would!"

"It will need a miracle like that," Jonathan Hayes agreed. "This man Cook is a thoroughgoing scoundrel—a free-lance trader, liar, thief, and murderer. His dirty, black schooner is the lawless terror of Aleut villages and lonely ranches over a thousand miles of this coast. But he's shrewd and plausible too, and he's kept pretty free of the revenue-cutter people and Federal prison. He's been after my secret for a year. Today, early, he got his men ashore at the far end of the island, unnoticed. My Aleut boys, luckily, saw them and brought me word before they surprised us. We weren't able to drive them off, but we may hold out here—I don't know."

"And if they do get into this house?"

Hayes answered significantly: "If they do, it won't be—*nice.*" The hint suggested more than a volume of description.

Marion burst out: "What's to become of me!"

He said soberly: "I don't know. You will take your chances— like the rest of us. I'd be a scoundrel, Miss Reade, if I didn't warn you that Cook is a bad lot and that his men are worse."

The warning unnerved her for a moment. Her immediate reaction from fright was to disbelieve what he had said. It was a story too fantastic for belief.

"Tosh!" she said, with all the scornful wisdom of her years and environment. "They only do things like that in the movies. This man Cook won't dare touch me!"

Hayes looked her over in appraising, disapproving silence. "They do things like that in places like this," he said slowly. "If you won't believe that, you're a fool. This man Cook will dare anything."

As if his words had been the signal, there came a scattering rain of shots, the thud of bullets against the plank shutters, and the answering volley from the riflemen close by the house.

Hayes sprang to his feet and left the room at a run.

The Aleut woman picked up a rifle and took up a position at a rear window. Marion Reade covered her ears, as if by denying her senses she could deny the reality of her peril.

CHAPTER III

"WHERE IS BROADWAY?"

JONATHAN HAYES CAME back within five minutes, during which a few scattering shots had been exchanged. Marion ran across the room to meet him.

"What is it?" she whispered. "Are they coming?"

All unconsciously she clung to his arm with both hands, looking up into his face like a frightened child. Hayes disengaged her hands with a reassuring smile and shake of the head.

"My boys see ghosts in the thickening dusk," he explained. "The waiting makes them jumpy. One fired at a shadow, and that started Cook's crowd. They're just as jumpy as we are, I dare say. I don't expect a real try for the house for an hour or more, until it's darkest."

Hayes spoke to the Aleut, evidently to the same purpose, and the woman grunted, but did not give up her position at the window.

"She's like what I have heard of the bulldog," he smiled at Marion. "She was told to watch that window for a possible attack from the rear—and I can't get her away from it."

The way he said it provoked a question Marion meant to ask. Had he never seen a bulldog? How silly!

But Hayes was reminded of something that put the question out of her mind.

"Can you handle a rifle?" he asked.

"I have shot one—a few times."

"Good enough! I'll post you at the other rear window, in the adjoining room, to help out Anna. Cook's men are in front and probably will attack that way. To reach the rear they must risk coming dangerously close to my boys. But it *could* be done, and I've got to guard against surprise. I'll get you a spare rifle, and if you see anybody, shoot. You can do that?"

"Kill them!"

"If you can shoot straight enough for that. I hope you can."

"Oh!" said Marion, her eyes round and big.

"It's their lives—or ours, you know!"

She swallowed hard and nodded.

"All right. Don't let it worry you now. You needn't take your post until I tell you. Lots of time yet. Sit down. Shall we talk about something pleasant?"

"Can—you think—of anything—*pleasant?*" Marion asked so intensely that he chuckled.

"Of course. Why not? Would you mind wrapping the seal-skins around you again—the way you had them? You looked so lovely." He picked up a pelt and placed it about her shoulders. He admired the effect in silence for several minutes, then said seriously, "It's so beautiful it makes me understand a little better. So beautiful—it almost excuses—women wanting them. I never imagined they would look—like that!"

He rose and brought her the small mirror and held it while she preened, forgetting her fears in her vanity. She laughed with pleasure and held the silky fur against her cheek.

"I'm glad you like them," said Hayes. "Because, if we get out of this, I want to give them to you—"

"Give them! You mean you would give me this skin?"

"That and as many others as you want. Remember, I have plenty—and shall never use them—"

"But I couldn't do that. I—we're not even acquainted. I couldn't take such a gift!"

"Acquainted! That's another thing. Sit down. Let's get ac-quainted." Hayes dragged up a chair to face hers and leaned forward, all interest. "Who are you? What are you? This New York you live in, that's a city, isn't it? What sort of place is it? What sort of world is it you live in—outside there? If you knew how I sat looking at you lying unconscious in that bed, wondering all these things, longing for the chance to ask them!"

His questions and exclamations poured forth so eagerly she was left confused. "You're too fast for me! One question at a time and I'll tell you everything I know, even my right age. Now!"

"Tell me about yourself. Please!"

"You needn't beg for that. Talking about myself is the best thing I do. I'm a publicity person, you know."

Evidently he did not know. The words might have been so much gibberish.

"Yes, I do high-class publicity. Not advertising, nothing like that, though I don't mind admitting to you that I got my humble start writing the copy for a hick town chemist out in Indiana who sold a beauty lotion by mail order. But that's my dark past and I try to forget it. Now I specialize in personal publicity, very different from mere advertising. I put over new musical comedy stars, society dames who go in for careers, explorers looking for angels to back their expeditions, humanitarians who want to reform the world—any and all kinds who have a yearning to see their pictures in the papers, their names in the electric lights or their reputations the talk of Broadway—" She stopped suddenly, halted by the look on his face. She exclaimed, "You poor dear! I don't believe the man has the slightest notion what I'm talking about!"

Hayes looked apologetic. "I seem to get a scrap here and there, but—"

"You never heard of publicity? Never heard of a press agent?"

Hayes shook his head. "What is—publicity?"

It was Marion's turn to look bewildered. She thought a moment and said, complacent of her definition, "Publicity is the life blood of Broadway."

"Just what," said Jonathan Hayes, "is Broadway?"

Marion's small figure stiffened with resentment. "That's cheap wit!" She was scornful.

"Wit? I don't understand—"

"If you think you can kid me let me tell you I've been kidded by experts!"

Plainly he was all at sea. His bewilderment was honest. He said apologetically, "If I said anything rude—I—beg your pardon—"

Marion leaned forward, breathless and stern. "You sit there and tell me you never even heard of Broadway?"

"I never did."

She couldn't doubt he told the truth. "Well—well, where have you been? You speak English. I suppose you read—and write?" He nodded. "You look—well, intelligent. Where *have* you been all these years?"

"On Kalvik Island," Hayes said. "On Kalvik. Nowhere else in the wide world. You don't believe that? It's the truth. When you talk to me like that, about the cities, about the life that goes on outside, you might as well be talking Greek. You see, I don't know anything about what goes on—out there—in cities—in the world. I've never seen a city. I've never seen even Dutch Harbor. I never saw anything!"

She considered this with evident suspicion. It was too improbable for her to accept.

Hayes protested. "I'm not a liar. Perhaps I am a fool—though I never thought of it that way before. Consider me a fool, and tell me—about Broadway."

"You sit there cold sober, and tell me you mean that? That you've never even heard of Broadway? That you've never been away from—this?"

"That's true. I've never been into your world."

"Why?"

He made a gesture of helplessness. "I'm here. I found myself here. Most of my life I didn't know how to get away—and I'm not sure now that I want to. I used to think I did! That was when I first learned there was some other place to go—a world full of cities and wonders—lamps that light without fire; wires that carry men's voices over thousands of miles; pictures that move and act like life; machines that go without dogs or horses or reindeer to draw them; great towers built into the clouds; men who fly in the air; crowds and riches and beauty that I can't begin to believe even now. And women—well, at least I believe in the women. I've seen you!"

Marion was staring. The simplicity of the man and the sincerity of his manner forced her to believe him—and yet she didn't believe. It seemed too incredible to her Broadway mind.

"You mean to say you've never seen the world? Never seen—anything?"

"Nothing—or, yes, to be honest, I have seen one of the marvels. Several years ago the talking-machine reached even this little back water. The Indians are fascinated by them. They will trap and hunt and work and save without stint to get one. A friend of mine, an Aleut, sent all the way to Juneau for one. When it arrived I traveled a hundred and fifty miles to hear it."

The big man stopped to chuckle in appreciation of the humor of it.

"I don't suppose you can imagine what that meant to me. You must see things like that every day when even our Indians and the Eskimos are beginning to use them. And yet that journey, to me, was as wonderful as—well, as one of those old Crusaders going to gaze upon the Holy Grail—or a Mohammedan going to Mecca!

"A couple of dozen Indians squatted in a council house listening to the talking toy—and myself—the most amazed and credulous of them all!"

He laughed briefly. "It was only then that I believed—really believed in those other marvels I have heard about. I had imagined them travelers' lies. That little box convinced me."

Now she was sure he was making fun of her. Why, his air of composure, his well-poised appreciation of the story—his unusual English, free of slang and cheapness, like some fellow in a book—these things betrayed him for what he was, some sort of a highbrow trying to put over his idea of a joke.

Trying to tell her he didn't know as much about the world as an Aleut Indian! Where did he get that stuff?

And yet she was more than half convinced. If this was acting, the man was a master of sincerity. She watched him narrowly as he waited for her comment. His sketchy smile was simple and friendly. His dark eyes were guileless. And there was an underlying note of sadness, of tragedy in his narrative that stirred her to pity in spite of the sophistication that whispered, "Surely, you're not going to fall for that?"

"Sounds kind of foolish, doesn't it?" he asked.

"I—don't know. Look me in the eye. What are you—the missing link, or the Great Auk—some kind of a leftover from the stone-hatchet age—or what?"

"I suppose—I'm something like—that," Hayes admitted. "In education—experience—those things, a sort of stone-hatchet man. If you care to hear, I can explain it—"

Marion's eyes were sparkling. Publicity training, the show-man's instinct, suddenly presented Jonathan Hayes, of Kalvik Island, in a new light—a new and fascinating aspect. She interrupted him with her exclamation: "Sweet lady! The cave-man on Broadway! What a riot that would be!"

"I beg your pardon, you said—"

"An idea, that's all. But what an idea!" With shining eyes she leaned forward and for emphasis patted his arm. "Mr. Hayes, if you'll take my tip—follow my advice—I'm going to bring you to life—"

"Bring me to life!"

She laughed. "You don't know it, but you're dead—and have been dead all these years. Yes, you have! Why, you've never even heard of Broadway! Worse than dead, but I'm going to show you how to live!" Before she could explain further the brilliant idea that was flowering so rapidly in her quick imagination they were reminded that even life on Kalvik had its complications—complications that were decidedly inimical to the chances of their ever again taking up the question of Broadway.

Men's voices rose in a savage yell and the rifles began to talk across the dark.

This time the attack really had begun.

CHAPTER IV

CAPTAIN DARIUS COOK

HAYES STEPPED QUICKLY to the wall where a rifle hung on pegs, took down the weapon and a belt of ammunition for Marion, who accepted it mechanically, with the feeling that she was dreaming.

"You're sure you understand how to use this?"

"Yes—oh, yes! I—you want me to shoot them down, in cold blood?"

"In self-defense!" he said sternly. "Are you afraid?"

"I don't know! Yes—perhaps. I—I can't make head nor tail of all this! It's so unreal—so fantastic. How do I know I want to kill these men?"

Before Hayes could answer, the door in the room adjoining, through which he had gone previously to speak to his men, opened quietly and he sprang to it. Marion followed him hesitatingly.

The stooping form of a man, indistinct in the darkness, stumbled in, dragging something. He spoke a few brief, guttural words to Hayes and went out again, leaving his burden.

Marion saw that another human form lay on the floor, inert. Hayes was bending over it.

"Light a candle on the mantel and bring it here," he said.

She found the candle, lighted it and came back, handing it to Hayes. By its flicker Marion saw the face of one of the Aleuts, the skin a sickly yellow, a trickle of blood winding across the flat, high cheek bones.

"Is he—hurt—badly?" she whispered.

"No," said Hayes shortly; "he's dead."

"Oh!" she said in a quiet, stunned whisper, and stood staring until Hayes's hand on her arm roused her.

"Come here, this is the window you must watch. See, here's the porthole in the shutter. Stand close against it so no possible light from inside can betray you. Keep your rifle up—like this. And watch. Watch everything. Shoot if you think you see anything move. Bullets are cheap. Don't mind wasting them."

She whispered back, querulously, "It's dark! I can't see."

"You'll soon get used to the dark. Watch!"

"Where are you going?"

"Where I'm needed—outside."

"Hayes! I'm afraid—that I—am—scared!"

Hayes sighed like a man trying to curb his impatience. "Please! I must depend upon your help. Watch that window!"

"But I don't want to fight. I—I didn't come here to fight. I'm no gunman. This is your feud—not mine!"

His hands seized her by both shoulders, not very gently. In the dusk his eyes seemed to glow with an angry, terrible fire of their own generation.

"It is your fight! If you value your life—if you want to keep that pretty body of yours out of Cook's hands—and his men's! If that means anything to you, you'll fight—you little fool!"

He shook her roughly and hurried away. She heard him let himself out of the door.

Marion was left gasping, speechless with surprise and incoherent indignation. Yet the first effect of his words was to send her to her vigil at the shuttered window, as he had ordered.

But Jonathan Hayes was laying up troubles for the future. In their brief acquaintance he had chalked up a mighty big account—and Marion would not forget it!

At the rear of the house she heard the popping of rifles faintly. The noise ceased to lose its menace; ceased to mean anything personal. The house itself was so quiet she heard the muffled cough of the Aleut woman, Anna, standing at the window in the next room, separated by a plank partition.

Her eyes became used to the dusk and made out the broader details of a night landscape, seen through the port of the shutter.

There was a stretch of ground behind the house cluttered by rocks and low bushes that rose into hillocks silhouetted vaguely against a sky of misty gray. The outlines of a well curb became visible. Another mystery resolved itself into a rack where fish were hung to dry and cure in the Indian way. Marion made out the dim form of a plow and a harness dangling from a pole.

Recognition of these commonplace objects began to rob the view of its first weird suggestiveness, but they also heightened by contrast, the sense of the ridiculousness, the nonsense, the fantasy of her situation.

Why was she standing there, with a loaded rifle, watching for a human head to shoot at? Why, indeed?

She was Marion Reade, something of a person, rated by those who knew as a decidedly clever young woman, capable of earning a very good income by her brains. Marion Reade had no part with the danger and blood and dirt of this private feud raging on an island in a forgotten corner of the world.

And yet because chance had cast her ashore here this man Hayes considered he had the right to thrust a gun into her hands and order her about! He had dared to shake her roughly; he, a hick, a dumb-bell, a country clown who had never even heard of Broadway!

She would show this man which of them was a fool!

Yet a certain sense of responsibility, the knowledge he had conveyed to her that there was real danger to them all, kept her from deserting her post. But when this was over!

The rattle of shots increased. Here and there on the shutters and against the shake roof of the building came the "sput" of bullets burrowing into the wood.

Marion began to wonder fearfully what the issue would be, and choked, tense with fright.

Something had moved, was moving again, across the gray, broken ground outside the window.

Something else rose suddenly and was seen in silhouette against the dim sky—a man's head and shoulders.

She was conscious of training her rifle, but she could not fire it.

A sort of buck fever seized her. Her hands were fluttering. Her knees knocked together. Her mouth was dry and the tongue stuck to the palate. She was both hot and cold, and, as if it was a nightmare of the normal kind, no power on earth could crook her finger about the trigger.

The silhouetted figure lingered for a time that seemed ages. The man evidently was studying the rear of the building. Her rifle covered him squarely. She could follow him readily as he moved.

But the girl who had calmly lighted a cigarette and cocked up her boots in the launch in theatrical defiance of what seemed sure death, was afraid to pull the trigger.

In vain she tried, with her swelling, paralyzed tongue, to call out. She could not even whisper.

That sense of utter terror—terror that demoralized every fiber, robbing her of the use of her arms and legs and faculties, became an exquisite torture.

She was aware suddenly that the head had vanished from her view. For just a moment she wondered with a wonder born of her desire to wish it so, if she had not suffered a vision caused by overstrung nerves.

Anna had not fired, and the Aleut watched the same ground from the corresponding window of the next room. That seemed to prove Marion had been tricked by imagination. Anna had no nerves. If there had been men there why had she not seen them? Of course Anna did not look from the same angle that Marion had, but—

"Hayes! Anna—" she screamed.

The rifle was knocked from her hands by a convulsion that shattered window glass and burst in the wooden shutters. The blows of some heavy instrument, some battering ram of timber, thundered on the planks and tore them from their hinges with a crackling of wood and screech of strained iron bolts.

In a panic Marion groped for the fallen weapon, all the time calling on Hayes and Anna.

Anna's rifle now was adding to the din.

The thick bar that held the shutters closed dropped with a crash, one of its sockets tom from the wall. The shutters flew open.

At the same time the front door of the house opened and men came in with a rush. There was a fight by those who came first to close the door against their pursuers. Guns fired within the house made an ear-splitting din.

Through the broken rear window at Marion's side other men tumbled in, their leader carrying an electric torch.

For the moment she was overlooked in the rush forward. The front of the building was a small riot of milling men, shouts, rifle shots and confusion. Quiet came unexpectedly, a comparative quiet at least, enough so that she heard a nasal, high-pitched, cackling sort of laugh, and the words, "Got you, Hayes!"

Then somebody blundered against her in the gloom and she was wrapped in a terrible, bearlike embrace, crushed close against a man's rough coat, conscious of the sickening unpleasantness of the contact. "Here's somebody else," her captor shouted, and added suddenly, "Holy angels—a woman!"

"It's that squaw," someone explained.

"The hell it is"—another voice—"we got the squaw here!"

The torch flashed on them and came closer until Marion's half-blinded eyes could make out slight details of the man who held it. She was examined slowly, with thoughtful attention.

The same nasal voice that had triumphed over Hayes, but

subdued now to a gentle, mocking quiet, exclaimed, "A lady! Well, I am surprised."

"Cap's right," shouted one of the group that crowded about. "It's a woman wearing man's pants."

"Tut-tut," the man with the flashlight said, in his smooth tones. Then, addressing Marion: "These boys of mine are uncouth, I'm afraid. You mustn't mind their remarks about your attire. They mean well. And now, if you don't mind, just who are you?"

"You tell this brute to let go of me?" Marion choked angrily.

"Quite right! Let her go—she's not armed."

The girl was released. She stood at bay, glaring into the torch light, tense and straight, an oddly boyish yet womanly little figure with the bobbed gold hair flying about her face, her jacket half torn from her body, the silk shirt disheveled.

"If you please," said her questioner, more gently still, "I really must know who you are. I'll confess I had no idea you were here—"

"You'll find out who I am—and that I have plenty of power-ful friends if one of you touches me again!"

"Nobody shall touch you, dear lady. Nobody. You hear?" He addressed the others: "Treat her with respect—like the finest lady in the land—all of you."

"And I warn you now, the yacht's not far off," Marion went on. "When my friends get here—"

"The yacht? Ah, I see, you're the visitor who came in that launch! H-m! A disabled launch, adrift in the fog—lost from the yacht—I see! I hope, dear lady, you did not suffer serious inconvenience during your long exposure?"

"I'll tell you one thing, I suffered and won't forget. I sha'n't forget how you tried to murder me—and I'll see that you answer for it, Captain Cook!"

The hand holding the flashlight startled a little at the name, but the voice answered softly, "So you know me? Hayes's doing, no doubt. You refer to the stray shots that must have bothered you when the launch went on the reef—"

"To the deliberate and studied attempt to murder me—that kept me under fire for at least half an hour," Marion corrected.

"A mistake! A most deplorable mistake! Your attire suggested a man—and the fog heightened the illusion. I offer you the humble apologies of every man here!"

"And I warn you, if you and your men care anything about your liberty, get off this island. When my friends come—"

Cook laughed softly. "Well, well, we must consider that, too!" There was scorn patent in every tone. "And now, lights, boys! Everybody in the other room by the fire. Let's count noses. And somebody open those windows and doors and get the smoke out. The house is stifling." To Marion he added: "Please come with me. Some of these boys are a little unruly."

Several lamps were lighted in the large living-room where Marion had lain and come to consciousness of this weird new world of Kalvik Island.

She saw three of Hayes's Aleut riflemen, the still dead form that had been dragged in and two others who sat on the floor, their backs against the wall, doubled over and moaning from wounds. The parka of one of them was clotted with his blood. She could readily imagine the fourth, dead out there in the fog.

The woman Anna stood in a comer, and a man armed with a pistol stood guard over her. Anna's mouth was shut in a straight, tight line, and her black eyes glittered like jet beads.

And by the fire, tied to a chair, his arms lashed to its frame, his legs hobbled, was Hayes.

When she saw the big man so helpless, Marion's conscience forced her to admit that at least part of the blame for this was hers. She had acted the part of the traitor, trembling at the window, too frightened to do the thing he told her. Her weakness had betrayed him!

"Hayes!" she cried contritely. "Oh, Hayes. I know I'm to blame! They came so fast—I was scared—I couldn't make myself fire that gun. Hayes, I am sorry!" There was no reproach in Hayes's look. He shook his head and smiled sadly. "Fortune of war," he said. "I don't blame anybody."

"Right!" Cook's nasal voice approved. "Certainly none of us would blame a lady!"

The room was light now, and men were opening the shutters and the door. Marion examined Cook with heightened interest. Their fate was in his hands. Already she mistrusted his suave voice.

He was a man of perhaps forty-five, chunky and short. A few sparse hairs were pomaded and combed with comical vanity over a domelike head that was almost bald save for these plastered strands and a thin fringe of reddish hair about the base of the skull. An aggressive red-brown beard jutted from his chin; otherwise his face was smooth. Close-set, green-gray eyes snapped sharply from their web of wrinkles. A straight slit of a mouth gave him an appearance of ugly smugness. Cook affected the clothes of a man of taste. There was jaunty neatness in his conservative tie with its scarab pin, his silk shirt, his blue-serge trousers and neat shoes. The costume was a strange contrast to the nondescript outfits of his men in their denims and half-knee mukluks.

"Cook," Hayes said sternly, "let me give you some good advice. Let that girl alone. She's not in this—"

"She carried a rifle, by her own admission," Cook said, with quiet triumph.

"She's not mixed up in it," Hayes repeated. "She didn't fire a shot—"

"But my dear chap, I'm afraid that wasn't her intention! That was—er—a case of nerves, let us say."

"I'm telling you," Hayes growled. "If you as much as touch her—or let one of these filthy dogs of yours hurt her—you'll answer for it. Her friends—"

"Are on a yacht, yes! A yacht that is somewhere, we can scarcely doubt. But where is it! The Pacific's a big ocean, Hayes.

If you had ever stood on a little vessel, as I have, looking over that wide horizon for an island no bigger than a pin point, you could understand why I'm not worrying. Besides," he added, briskly, "we shall not be long."

He planted himself before Hayes.

"Wouldn't you like to tell me quietly just where those pelts have been cached?" he suggested.

"What pelts?"

"Oh, come! We admit there's a cargo of them, several schooner loads, accumulated and stored away safely in an ice cave. We both know that. Tell me where they are and I promise you in fifteen minutes we'll all be gone from here—and apologize for all the trouble we made you."

Hayes shook his head.

"Come, come! You refuse—"

"You—and your men—may go to hell."

"What! Before a lady? Such words! Think of the annoyance you can save by granting my reasonable request."

Hayes kept silent.

"Now, Hayes, you know I'm a man of my word!" Cook's head stuck forward aggressively. He stood with legs spread and neck extended, looking more ridiculous than deadly to Marion. "I always keep my word," Cook repeated. "You wouldn't listen to a good proposition. You wouldn't go halves with me. You were obstinate and greedy. I promised you I would come back some day and make you tell. I am back, Hayes. Look what my coming has cost you! The death of two of your men—four probably, since the other two are certain to die from their wounds in a few hours. Man, do you feel no remorse for that?"

"I do not," said Hayes. "My boys died like honest men—fighting for a good cause. I'm not afraid to die that way." Cook looked shocked. "Dear, dear, dear!" he said, affecting mild protest. "Let's not talk of such a thing. Hasn't there been violence enough? You have only—"

"Cook!" Hayes burst out angrily. "Be damned to you and your

lies! You pussy cat, standing there, licking your lips! Go ahead and make a Roman holiday out of me, but don't lie!"

Cook smirked and sighed. "I'm afraid this man is incorrigible!" he exclaimed, rolling his eyes about the room. "A bad case. And all I ask is to be friends with him!"

Hayes's body was convulsed with a frantic effort to break his bonds, an effort that rocked his chair and caused several men to spring forward threateningly. Cook waved them back with soft words. Hayes glared murder at him, and the bald-headed man only smiled gently.

"I only wished to be your friend," Cook repeated with mournful emphasis.

Hayes's face seemed almost to blacken with the rush of angry blood. "You—filthy—liar!" he growled.

"Don't!" Marion cried, laying her hand on his shoulders. "Oh, don't! Can't you see he's playing with you—like a cat with a mouse it has caught! Don't let his talk hurt you!"

The touch of her hand seemed to soothe the man to some sort of reasonableness. "You're right," he mumbled.

Cook said, a little more severely, "I must ask you not to interfere, dear lady. Will you please step away from that chair, or—" He had her by the arm, gently urging her to one side. Marion shuddered at his touch, but she moved away, knowing it was the only way to avoid something worse. She began to tremble violently and felt a dreadful nausea.

"You must not speak to him again," Cook was saying to her. "Really, I must insist on that! And I am master of ceremonies here!"

He turned again to face Hayes, still softly ingratiating of manner. "Consider, Hayes. Is it wise to provoke more trouble? Is the secret worth it? These seal pelts—they're no more yours than mine. They were hid in the days when the Pribilof rookeries were being raided daily by men who were no better than pirates. The men who stole them first are dead, killed in a fight with the revenue cutter people, and the pelts forgotten; they're anybody's who can get them. And you told me in your own words that *you didn't want them*. Your motive seemed a little odd to me, but I don't doubt your sincerity. Then why act the dog in the manger? Tell me where they are; I can use them, and you will be no worse off—"

Hayes was shaking his head steadily. "You'll never learn from me!"

"In your own words there has already been too much violence and bloodshed over these skins, Hayes. Would you cause more?"

"I'm not afraid of you!"

Cook's voice became more businesslike, harder. "Then all I've got to say is, I'm sorry for you! Boys, is that branding iron hot?"

A man, watching the hearth, bent down and drew out from the coals a long iron poker that glowed almost at white heat, snapping off showers of tiny sparks. He handed it to Cook.

The captain, who had first daintily turned back the silk cuff from his wrist, advanced close to the helpless prisoner until the iron glowed hot against Hayes's face.

Marion Reade knew that she was screaming—a mad screech of unadulterated terror. She thought she was going mad.

CHAPTER V

THE YACHT

AS MARION SCREAMED another thing happened.

The Aleut woman, Anna, struck out with her fist and felled the man who guarded her. She was across the long room with a bound and had seized Cook, pinioning his arms. In the scuffle he was thrown against the iron. There was a moment's sickening smell of scorching cloth and flesh. Cook shrieked.

That shrill cry from their captain seemed to rouse the others from the stupor Anna's boldness had cast them into. They tore the squaw away from Cook. Several rifles and pistols were raised to kill her.

Cook's words stopped the imminent murder. "Wait!" he ordered. "Not here! Hold that woman a minute!"

He thrust the hot iron back among the coals and addressed himself to Anna in Aleut. He stood close to her, head thrust out, face pallid with pain and rage, and the spitting gutturals of his harangue were poisonous with hate and deviltry.

Anna paled as she listened. When Cook had finished she made a curt answer, evidently defiant.

"Take her outside, back of the house!" Cook directed. "We'll have no killing here."

Several men led Anna away. Over her shoulder she said something to Hayes in her own tongue, something that brought a tortured groan from the big man. To Cook he burst out, "You are a dirty, murdering cur, aren't you? Killing helpless women is the best thing you do!"

"One of the best things," Cook agreed, managing a smile of a sort. "And that reminds me—this other young lady—"

"I warn you, Cook!"

"My dear chap, you do misjudge me so! I wouldn't dream of hurting one so charming." He managed a smirking bow to the white, terrified girl. "Dear lady, this is no place for you. Men's quarrels were never meant for your hearing. You must let me take you outside. Really the sunrise is lovely so near the Arctic Circle!"

He urged Marion gently, his hand at her elbow, and she involuntarily took a step or two, avoiding the touch.

Then she stopped. "I won't go," she exclaimed. "If you mean to murder me like Anna, kill me here."

"Please, please—You don't know how badly such evidence of mistrust hurts me. Nobody means to do you harm. From now on you are our honored guest. My schooner will be at your disposal. But you must come outside, as I ask. It's not a place for a tender girl, in here. I wouldn't have you see. And surely"— a threat was suggested now—"surely, you won't make me insist!"

"Hayes!" Marion cried. "Hayes!"

"For God's sake, go outside!" Hayes groaned.

Still she hesitated. She turned on the staring men from Cook's schooner. They were a hard looking lot, men whose faces were marked with beastliness, murderous excitement, inhuman resolution. "Isn't there one man in this room?" she asked. "Not one man with the honesty and courage to stop this torture and murder? Will no man help him?"

"You must go," Hayes said sternly. "Go now, Miss Reade. And if you believe in God, ask Him to help you—and ask Him to have mercy on my soul."

"Come," Cook said soothingly. "Come with me. You are unstrung—ill. Why, you're shivering!" He snatched the rough, warm mackinaw coat from the man nearest him and threw it cape-wise about her slender shoulders. He led her gently a little distance from the house.

At his beckoning one of the men followed them.

"This man will stay near you, but he will not speak to you nor bother you in any way," Cook said with an emphasis meant for the guard. "I will soon have my little business finished. Then we must all go away—and forget this—unpleasantness—in happier thoughts."

The world had turned luminous. There was a thin mist that glowed and pulsed with color, the glory of the rising sun. Cook lingered a moment, facing the wonder of a new day. He sighed in a sort of ecstasy.

"What color! What a miracle of light! You forget there is beauty like that, you who watch the cheap lights and tinsel of Broadway, Miss Reade."

Marion stared at the man and saw by his face he was utterly sincere for the moment. He stood like a primitive worshiper of beauty, awaiting the rising sun.

Somehow his intoxication with beauty made him seem more terrible than ever.

"But it never lasts—no beauty lasts," Cook sighed. "Look, it's paling now. Like that lupine there, born only to fade." He plucked a spray of the blue lupine and crushed its flower in his hands.

"Poor, fragile beauty!" He dropped the mangled spray. With that he turned back to the house, toward his work of torture and murder.

There was something about this man with his almost comic figure and face, his gentle, whining voice and poet's love of beauty, and his cold-blooded, ruthless, greedy cruelty that was out of the course of nature and abominable. Marion felt it and watched him go with a shudder.

What of Hayes, and what of her future? She dared not think ahead. She dared not think at all. She began to pace back and forth nervously. The man left to guard her offered no objection, himself following her pacing, but at a respectful distance.

The place where she stood was a rise of ground some little

distance from the log house. It was open country, like all the
island, rolling, broken ground with many rocks and a growth
of low bushes. Only in the sheltered hollows were there trees
of any size, cedar and spruce, stunted and often twisted by the
sea winds.

She could see the island for some distance about, the open
sea partly visible in the thin mist, where the sun was rising,
gilding the white water of the surf that grew and vanished in
the haze like some dissolving picture; the bush-clad, broken
little hills and ridges; the cliffs where, at some distance, a man
was standing, evidently one of Cook's men on watch; the solid,
square log house of Jonathan Hayes, sheltered from the sea by
a low ridge.

Toward the house she began to stare in a fascination of terror.
It was there a man would be tortured to death—a big, fine chap
who had been kind to her. There she had seen a woman con-
demned to death—and any moment might bring to her ears
the report of the shots that killed her—and Cook was there,
the man who would dispose of her future as he pleased.

This was reality. She could not deny it now by pretending
she dreamed. No amount of her city sophistication could laugh
it off. New world as it was to her, Kalvik Island, with its fantastic sequence of events, was real; she was vitally concerned.

Marion Reade wished with all her heart that she might fall
dead or go mad—anything to lose all responsibility and sense
of her connection with these things.

She started at a new and different sound.

At first she thought it the shots of men in or near the house,
but these reports were more distant. Then a shrill whistle like
a boar's call, began to blow. She saw that her guard had turned
a startled face toward the distant man on the cliff.

This watchman was running toward them. His whistle kept
shrilling, and she saw him raise a pistol and fire more shots in
rapid succession, aiming into the air. Evidently a signal.

A shout came from the log house. A few of the men ran out;

then came Cook and several more. They hurried toward the watchman from the cliff. Marion's guard began to run, cutting at an angle which would join the group. The girl was left alone, some distance from them all.

The log house emptied more now, evidently all of the outlaws. She saw them gesticulating, pointing toward the sea.

"The yacht!" she whispered to herself and strained her eyes at the rising clouds of fog. She saw nothing, yet evidently Cook and his men did.

They began to move rapidly, almost at a run, across the bare hills toward the opposite side of the island. They paid no further attention to Marion.

She ran toward the cliff, to see what had driven them away. The sun was above the horizon now and daylight made things that had been mysterious a few moments before commonplace. The mist had thinned. Out along the horizon, at last, she made out a tiny white shape that sent up a plume of smoke. It was no bigger than some distant gull, drifting on the waves, but it sent up its steady, twisting thread of smoke, and it moved with a purpose. She had no glass, as Cook's man had, to examine it, but she knew it for a vessel, a vessel headed for the island, and she guessed it was the *Frivolity*.

She looked and looked until her tired eyes refused to see any more. She laughed and cried at the same time.

A thought of Hayes recalled her to sanity. Cook's men had disappeared. She was alone. There was no sound save the rumble of surf on the reef and the crying of a gull, fishing among the breakers.

Whether Hayes was alive or dead she did not know. She turned toward the log house. As she neared it she noted the opened shutters, the gaping door. It had a strange, abandoned, lifeless look that frightened her.

CHAPTER VI

A WOMAN OF TINSEL

AT THE DOOR of the log house Marion stopped. She was trembling, and her mouth was dry with a new sort of fear. She dreaded to look into that quiet place, afraid to see what Cook had done to his prisoner, afraid of the dead Aleut she already had seen, and those ghastly wounded men crumpled against the wall like empty sacks.

In spite of her fear and nerves she was wildly impatient to know the fate of Hayes. She made herself go in the door, turning her eyes resolutely from the Aleuts who lay as she last saw them, and going directly to the big room.

In the doorway she gave a glad cry, "Hayes! Oh—you're safe! It's—all right? Oh, thank God!"

She leaned weakly in the door, almost hysterical with happiness.

Hayes was there, unharmed, in the chair he had been bound to, and the Aleut woman, Anna, was kneeling beside him, a sharp knife in her busy hands, cutting the cords that bound him.

"Safe enough!" Hayes answered with a grin. "There, don't get upset about it."

"And Anna, too! I—I thought—that she—"

Hayes's eyes flashed. He addressed Marion proudly:

"Kill Anna? Why, she has got more nerve than Cook and all his men. They took her behind the house to shoot her, one man holding her and two others raising their rifles to fire, and she threw the man that held her straight in their faces— Wonder their shots didn't kill him! It was a lively row for five minutes, and that five minutes was long enough to keep that devil from marking me up with his branding iron. I tell you this woman Anna is worth more than all the gold in Alaska!"

Hayes added a few words of Aleut, evidently to the same effect, for the benefit of the squaw. Anna only grunted, but her black eyes glittered strangely, and there was a momentary softening of her wrinkled face. She cut the last of the bonds and stood impassive again.

Jonathan Hayes stretched his legs and arms and rose. His arms went about the Aleut and drew her to him. He bent his head and kissed her tenderly.

"There's a real woman for you!" he exclaimed fondly. "And she can fight like a whole regiment of soldiers."

"Uh," said Anna, who evidently gathered the sense of this remark without translation.

Marion Reade felt herself very small, neglected and lonely. She had come to him all emotion, and in the joy of finding him alive she could have clasped him in her arms and kissed him herself. But Hayes forgot her completely to shower his praises on a middle-aged squaw—a savage Aleut, fat, dowdy, fishy, with a face like a Hallowe'en mask!

In her heart she knew she deserved the neglect. Anna had fought, risked her life, given everything to help Hayes. Marion had whined, shirked, finally betrayed him. It was justice.

But the justice of it—though she could recognize it—did not alleviate the bitterness of her surprise at the demonstration, nor her hurt at the neglect. If Hayes would give her only a word of praise! For some reason she found herself craving it. But Hayes failed to give it.

The big man released Anna suddenly. "Now about those wounded boys—" he began.

"The yacht is coming!" Marion interrupted eagerly. "It did come, as I said! It saved us. Hayes, come out and look at it!"

"Yacht? Oh, yes, of course! I supposed that must be it when Cook gave up so suddenly. Night birds like Cook are easily scared off!"

She seized his hand eagerly. "Come, look—it's so lovely!" she begged.

"The yacht will keep." Hayes turned away. "There are men suffering in that other room—my own Aleut boys, Anna!"

The two of them went to the wounded men and Marion followed slowly, feeling entirely out of it.

Nobody seemed to care a hang about her or the yacht. But it was her doing, that yacht. She'd like to know where they all would have been if it hadn't come! She decided with anger born of her pique that before she left the island this big hick would remember she was on earth—yes—and be eating out of her hand, too! She'd make him suffer!

She tried to help in giving first aid to the wounded Aleuts, but found herself very much in the way. She was glad to slip away from unpleasant sights. She wandered about the big room and came upon her vanity case, left lying since she had quit the blankets in that dim, almost forgotten evening before.

She snapped open the cover and examined herself in the small mirror with eager interest. Had she aged terribly? She had heard that awful experiences like these turned people's hair white! Sweet lady! Suppose her hair—No, that was all right, at least. How about frightful wrinkles? Well, there wasn't anything very serious. Looked pretty rocky, of course—like a fried egg, she called it, but nothing that couldn't be remedied.

She sat down in the best light and began to remedy these things methodically.

In her mirror she caught sight of Hayes, standing in the doorway, watching her. She concealed the knowledge, ignoring him completely. Was he frowning disapproval? She hoped so. Marion began to hum a gay little tune as she worked. She would ignore him until he spoke. That always put a man at a disadvantage, having to start things.

"Suppose," Hayes said presently, "we go look at your yacht now? Everything's all right here. I'll get my glass."

"Oh—yes," Marion murmured. "Just a minute." She worked on for several minutes.

"Do you always do—that?" Hayes asked finally. He had a marine glass and was waiting to go.

"What—this?"

"Yes. Is that so—necessary?"

"In my young life it is," she said cheerfully, intent on emphasizing an eyebrow with which nature already had done her artistic best.

Hayes did not say anything, but she knew he was thinking something disapproving. Finally she exclaimed, "Oh, you're waiting? So sorry to keep you!"

She went out with him, her hand tucked under his arm, skipping gayly. "Run!" she commanded. "Run quick, to the beach. It looks so pretty, sailing to rescue us!"

"Must have seen our beacon fire," Hayes murmured, complying a little awkwardly with the command to run.

The vessel was much closer, evidently headed straight for Kalvik, now. Hayes handed her the glass. "Is that your friends?"

"Yes! It's Fox—and Beach, and Ada, and Al. All of them! Oh, oh!" She began to wave a very small handkerchief with a pretty, frantic sort of enthusiasm. For purposes of signaling, at that distance, the performance was quite useless.

Hayes took the glass and examined the oncoming yacht. "No wonder Cook's men were scared!" he exclaimed. "That yacht looks a lot like the revenue cutter *Bear!* At a distance it would be hard to find the difference. There aren't many cutters in Alaska waters, but what there are of the revenue men certainly do make life hell for Cook and his like. That probably explains why he didn't murder me in cold blood as a parting revenge. He wasn't going to add one little item to the count against him. A canny man, Cook!"

"Don't ever mention that man's name!" Marion cried, sobered

completely. "I never dreamed a human being could be so—so utterly frightful." She shivered violently.

"We won't mention him again," Hayes assured her. "There, don't think about it—"

"I won't. I don't care. I don't care about anything now. I'm safe. We're both safe. The yacht's come back, hurrah, hurrah!" She sang it in her exultation. "I'm going home, home, home again—back to Broadway!"

She saw Hayes's expression sober quickly and was glad as she read his thoughts. "I don't suppose," she mused impishly, "that you'll ever miss me—or even think of me again!"

"I shall miss you." He said it grimly.

"And you really are going to stay on this island—on Kalvik? You mean you're going to spend the rest of your life here?"

"What else should I do?"

"You're rich, aren't you? Those sealskins—"

"I might get those sealskins, if I had a large vessel," Hayes said. "And I suppose they could be turned into money. Perhaps a lot of money. I'm not quite sure that I want it. What good is money on Kalvik—"

"Don't stay on Kalvik. Come with us. Let me show you what real living is like—the way people live in the world!"

Hayes shook his head slowly. "I'm not sure—but I like Kalvik—pretty well."

Marion stared about her, at the house built securely in the hollow protected from gales; at the barren rolling hilltops of the island where only the hardy bushes lived among the rocks; at the little groves of huddling fir and spruce in the hollows. All of it had a bleak, hard bitten look. Life survived here, but only through everlasting struggle against wind and sea.

The Broadway product shivered in the chill air, and catching Hayes's arm, snuggled close.

"You mean to say you *like* this place?" she demanded.

"I mean to say it's all the world I know," Hayes said. "And—

yes—I like it now. But there was a time, a few years, when I hated it. God, if you could realize how I longed to get away from this! Now, when I could go, I'm not so sure I care to."

She looked hard at him, curiously, beginning to speculate. This was a queer sort of man—and she had not forgot that in some way he might be made useful to her.

"Sit down on this rock," he said. "Take a look round and see if you can put yourself in my place. This is all the world I re-member. I was not born here, but when I came I was too young to know the difference. My father told me about that. He was a minister, a queer sort, I guess. He had some sort of row with the people outside, back there in the States where his ministry was. I don't even know the name of the place. He was a widower then. He took me and came away. He came here, by choice, as far from all that life as he could get. He built this house and got fields under cultivation and made friends of the few Aleuts who had a little village over there in the cove.

"And this was my world. I knew nothing else, and being a boy, didn't care about anything else. I was taught to read and write by my father. The rest of life I learned from the Indians— and I learned it well. I can handle a bidarka in any kind of weather. I can spear a walrus or seal with the best of them. I know the fishing and the hunting, and I can make a fair job of sewing a parka or mukluks. I know about some of the herbs that make good medicine, too. I can take care of myself all right. That's a lucky thing, because I've had to most of my life!

"My father died when I was twelve. You can see his grave over there behind the house, if you're curious. The Indian woman, Anna, looked after me then, and I grew up pretty much among her people. I think, perhaps, I did them some good.

"You can't know these Aleuts as I know them. Let me tell you they are good clear through! Honest people, industrious, sober when they're left alone by the whites. They are loyal friends. My father advised them often, about housing and their health and the Great Spirit. They brought their quarrels to him for settlement. After he died they got to depend on me. Seemed to think the gift was passed on from father to son. You see, I am not the least important person on Kalvik!"

Marion pressed his arm. "You poor lamb!" she murmured, and her eyes were moist. "You poor, lonely lamb!"

"Hunh!" said Jonathan Hayes, scorning pity. "I was all right."

"But you must have wanted to get away! Didn't you long for white faces; to be among your own kind of people?" Hayes's jaw twisted and his mouth became grim.

"Yes, I did," he said, looking far out to sea. "There was a time when it nearly drove me out of my head. I knew there was another world, you see. There were the books my father left— and confirmation of what they said in occasional stories that traveled among the Aleuts, tales of the white people and their world. We're far out of it here, of course—'way off the beaten track; but the gold discoveries brought thousands; then the traders and fishers came, and the word spread, and gradually I realized there was a world of my kind of people—and all of a sudden I knew I was lonely—utterly, damnably lonely!

"I could have gone away, of course. I started to go several times, but something interfered. My friends, the Aleuts, would get sick and send for me. There were things to be done here. It didn't seem fair, somehow, to abandon the place my father had picked for home. And I was afraid, too—afraid of this civilized world I had read about and heard about. I wasn't fitted for it. I would have died in it an untrained man, absolutely incapable of fitting into it without money to help me. And then, just as if my prayers had been answered, I found all the money a man could ask for."

"Well," Marion exclaimed humorously, "I didn't realize I was visiting a millionaire!"

"A millionaire? Well, I don't know. I'm rich enough, anyhow, or could be if I pleased."

She examined him curiously. He evidently believed what he said. There was only one way to take him—without a smile.

"Sweet lady! Now, I suppose, you're going to add that you don't please?"

"You're right. I don't believe that I do."

"Humph! I won't say I don't believe you—"

"Why should you?"

"Why, indeed! Only make a note of this, will you? Don't talk in your sleep—or anything—while I'm around. I'd hate like sin to know where you keep your million. After all, I'm only a frail woman—and I'd hate to be tempted. Money! What I'd do to get my hands on it—"

Hayes laughed. "Your two little hands couldn't carry off enough to worry me. Because it's not money—it's those seal skins. And I intend to give you all you want, anyhow."

He began staring out to sea again, forgetting her. Marion stirred uneasily, coughed several times with pointed emphasis, hummed a little tune. Finally she said: "Well, of course, my dear, I'm not curious. Oh, no! I'm not the curious type of female at all, and mercy knows I wouldn't pry into your affairs! *But*—"

"Oh, it wasn't anything—much. It was this way. Years ago, back in the nineties, schooners used to raid the seal rookeries on the Pribilof Islands—that's up to the north of here—north and west—out toward Siberia. The herds were plentiful then, and the guards didn't amount to much, and a smart skipper who was willing to take chances could pick up what was a fair fortune even in those days of cheap skins.

"I don't know the exact details, but one man who was bolder and more successful than any of them—a man whose greed knew no bounds—much like this man Cook—raided and raided again and overtaxing the capacity of his schooner found a safe place to hide his loot in a bay over on the peninsula, a bay that lies under a mountain where a big glacier comes down to the sea. There are ice caves there, and the rough-cured pelts were hid in them—a great accumulation, placed in natural cold storage.

"The raider was caught finally, disabled by a storm that had drowned most of his men. The survivors were sent to a federal prison for long terms.

"An Indian, a friend of mine, found the cache of skins. He told me of it, and I have seen the place. The pelts are packed in the ice, as good today as they ever were. You have seen some. Anna and her sister cured those skins, scraped them, picked out the long hairs with infinite patience. Experts among her people call them prime pelts—and they know!

"That's my fortune, Miss Reade. A big one, I think. But it would need a pretty big ship to carry it away. When I first saw it I was all enthusiasm. I saw in it my deliverance from Kalvik. I meant to venture into your world and find somebody with a ship who would take a share in the skins for his services. Then I changed my mind, one day—"

"And what changed your mind?"

"Cook!" Hayes answered bitterly. "Cook heard about those skins. I think it likely one of those men who survived the wreck of the raider and were sent to prison gave the secret to him. That is most likely, because Cook does not know the location of the bay—and a common sailor would be unable to give it to him. Also, jail-birds are the sort of company Cook would fancy!

"Cook, then, was my first introduction to the civilization you seem so fond of. He bore out most of the stories I have heard about that sweet world you live in!" Hayes's tone was savagely contemptuous.

Marion's tone was also scornful as she exclaimed: "Cook! You think him a fair sample? You think civilization is made up of men like that!"

"I have reason to think it," Hayes answered. "Cook is a fair average of what civilization sends to these shores. That gang from outside, traders, prospectors, fishers, whalers! Do you know what their greed has done to Alaska, to the simple, honest natives? Their touch is like the touch of leprosy. Wherever their feet step a blight is left behind. Men and children die. Women are outraged. That's the history of my country, the history of my friends, the Aleuts, wherever the whites have come. Greed! That's the keynote of it, greed and violence and murder. And when I saw Cook, that vile thing brought it home to me. Why should I sell these pelts—mine perhaps by right of discovery— but stolen just the same? What good would they do? Feed the vanity of painted, pampered, useless women; generate new crimes and greed and bloodshed! What good is there in that for me? I'll stay here—clean-handed."

His vehement declaration left Marion momentarily over-whelmed. The man's great simplicity and sincerity were beyond question. He meant all that he said. Never had she met an idealist like this, nor even believed there could be such a one! His innocence left her baffled. The arguments she could think of would turn aside from their point as if he were armored.

Because it seemed more difficult to get, having her way with this man became vastly more important. She would take him to the world he derided, straight back to Broadway, or know the reason why. And once she got him there, in her own proper environment, she would tame this cave man of Kalvik Island. That would be something worth talking about!

Yet how to convince him—win him?

"But you don't know. You don't understand!" she exclaimed earnestly. "I don't know how to tell it. You have to see and feel it to realize it. But, my friend, believe you me, if you haven't seen New York, if you haven't seen Broadway, you simply have not been born!" She considered this and nodded. "That's it, you haven't begun to live yet. All those other years are just junk. Think of it! Buildings that stick 'way up into the sky, their towers glistening with gold. A huge, wonderful city of them, stretch-ing for miles. And at night the lights, like your Northern Lights, every color and shape, dancing and winking and glaring. Mil-lions of people. You get a thrill out of just that, the way they stream past you, all movement and talk and noise and excite-ment—it's the biggest thrill of all. And the shows—oh, boy! And the clothes! And the parties!" She then gave a sigh. "Oh,

I wish I could make a speech like yours and make you understand it!"

"I think you put it very well." Hayes smiled. "Yet what does it amount to? A house that reaches to the sky? That is only a house. A million people? I cannot know a million people; it is more than I can do to understand just one or two. Lights? I have a lamp here. Your lights are only that lamp multiplied many times. Clothes—and shows—and parties?" He shook his head.

Marion said seriously: "Those aren't the real things, the fine things. I know that. Just because I talk like a giddy flapper you mustn't think I don't know good things. How about the wonderful music? How about fine paintings and statuary and great buildings filled with all the great books the world has produced? How about association with the people who are doing all the big things—and the encouragement they give you to think and to do for yourself? Can you get such inspiration here?"

"Good! That's better. Now you have me half convinced. Tell me some more about these advantages."

Marion's brows knitted. "I—well, I don't know how. You have to see for yourself. And—I might as well be honest, I don't know much about such things." She smiled eagerly. "But we could find out—together."

Her words and smile startled him a little.

His hands rose as if to touch her, but he dropped them at his side and began to frown. "No, I don't need your towns and streets and lights. I don't need your kind of life."

But now she understood the appeal to make. His suppressed gesture of interest betrayed the weakness in his armor. She glowed with satisfaction to know that she herself was the best argument of all! Now she knew how to triumph over this man who neglected her for an Aleut squaw!

"But you will come, won't you, Hayes—if I should wish you to come—if I should wish it very much? You'll come—to keep me—from being—lonely?"

As she said it she came closer to him, putting her hands on his arms. There was a tremulous smile on her lips as she raised her eyes to his. She knew this was the weapon to fell her cave man, and used it without thought of consequences.

Hayes's answer was sudden and startling. Those brown eyes, a little moist, turned to his; her face uptilted, her closeness in his arms, all of these did something to him as sudden and terrible as a rifle bullet. He saw her—then he saw her no more, but had caught her in his arms and swept her off her feet, his lips pressed against hers.

Marion was helpless in his savage grip; her universe danced and whirled in a kind of vague, dizzy measure, and still he did not let her go. She was too dazed by the suddenness of it to think coherently or find a way to protest. Then abruptly he had set her on her feet so roughly that she staggered.

Hayes spoke hoarsely, words even more astonishing than this kiss. "You beautiful, tinsel thing—so lovely—*and so damnably, utterly useless!* And, oh God! How I want you!"

She drew back slowly, a step or two. Her face was white. Something hard and bitter looked from her eyes—a look that seared and chilled him and made him an abject figure.

She said nothing, only looked for long minutes straight at him while he suffered. Then she turned away with studied deliberation and walked toward the beach.

Hayes, watching her small figure, straight and lithe and scornfully angry in every line, groaned in his crushing desire.

The yacht was dropping anchor in the bay.

CHAPTER VII

THE SUPREME DUMB-BELL

MARION READE HELD the center of the stage and all the spotlights in the bijou saloon of the yacht *Frivolity*. The recital of her adventures was exciting enough to hold a larger audience than this group of four, and she saw with practiced art that the recital lost nothing of its drama in her version.

She looked slight and frail in a big lounging chair, the center of a rough half circle of chairs that held her listeners. Mrs. Fox—"Ada"—sat close beside her, a statuesque woman of about forty, with chemically blond hair and a kindly, vacantly pretty face, who patted her hand often and called her "Dearie."

Douglas Fox sat next to his wife, a big, lumpy figure in tweed hunting-jacket and knickers, plaid wool stockings of conspicuous pattern, and a yellow camel's hair cap which he wore indoors and out in a manner that he conceived to be the spirit of the traditional English hunting squire. Fox was a truly fine figure run to fat; his smooth-shaved face was handsome in a heavy, fleshy way. His eyes were baffling, a light blue that suggested self-interest, but he enjoyed a great popularity. He sucked at a black shell-briar pipe as he listened.

Irving Beach, next to Fox, lounged without the peculiarly offensive aggressiveness of his host. He had the ease of a man born to lounging-chairs. Like Fox, he was big, but unlike Fox, kept in trim. His close-cut hair curled a little and was streaked with white. His eyes were gray and pleasant when he was interested, as he was just now, and a neatly trimmed mustache set off his aristocratic face. His hunting clothes were worn, but looked, somehow, more natural on their owner than did Fox's.

The fourth guest of the *Frivolity* was a short, thin, wiry, bald-headed person of undetermined age, with shrewd brown eyes, a wide, thin-lipped mouth and a nervous, shrill laugh. He was slangy and flash in dress and manner, and his comments exploded like the crackling of firecrackers. Al Sapley depended on comedy for his popularity. He was a great man for parties.

A Japanese boy in a white jacket was mixing cocktails at the sideboard. He worked at it with the serious, methodical manner of a man who knew exactly the task ahead of him at that hour and on this occasion.

"Now listen," said Marion, "I've saved the best of this to the last. I'm going to show you something tonight at dinner that's worth the whole trip. I've discovered something. I've discovered something so good that, Douglas, you are going to agree with me it's worth even the price of your launch that I lost—"

"You should worry about that launch!" Fox protested with a wave of his pipe.

His wife added: "We've got you back, dearie. God knows we don't care what that cost!"

"I said all the time we were looking, I'd spend every red cent Doug Fox owns to get our sweetie back." Al Sapley barked.

Marion bowed mockingly. "I am but the dust under my lord's feet! But don't think I haven't done something to show you my gratitude. Let me tell you about what I found on this island. It's going to surprise you—"

Mrs. Fox interrupted ecstatically: "Was it that man, dearie?"

Sapley cried: "Ada said it. Of course it's a man—"

"It was—and it."

"Who, this Drake—Mayes—Hayes, whatever his name is?" Fox protested. "I don't see anything about him—"

"Wait! Listen, all of you. This is good. You only met him a minute on the beach. I staged that. I'm saving him for dinner, when he can make his entrance right. Don't get the idea you're going to see any ordinary backwoods John. You're not. I found something Barnum would have jumped at, I tell you. Ladies, and Bitter Halves, I am going to introduce to you tonight in the person of Jonathan Hayes, of Kalvik Island, the one and only living survival of the ice age—the human Great Auk—the last surviving member of the famous Stone-hatchet family of this U.S.A.—the man who never saw nothing, don't know nothing, and is proud that he don't. I am going to show you the Supreme Dumb-bell of the Universe!"

The girl's tongue rattled into the story of Jonathan Hayes, of Kalvik. She sketched it for them much as Hayes had told it to her. But unlike in Hayes's, in her telling, it got all its dramatic value. It leaped at their attention and clinched it with all of the verbal punctuation and red ink phrases at her command. She made them listen and she made them appreciate it. She summed up finally:

"You get the idea, do you? A man who never saw an electric light or a permanent wave. He's stepped right out of the days when they used to chase the dinosaurs off the cave doorstep every morning—and he's worth a million or more. The man who could buy Broadway—and wouldn't even know how to buy an ice cream soda. And he's mine! Mine by right of discovery!"

"Now look here, Marion," Sapley broke in, "do you mean to say, on the level, this John of yours never even saw one of these Alaska hick towns—"

"Never saw anything! I'm telling you—"

"And worth billions—"

"Well, something like that—"

"Wow!" Sapley shouted in his cracking voice, waving his arms as he faced them. "An Alaskan billionaire that never even learned how to buy a subway ticket, a hick that sheds gold dust instead of hayseeds—and our Marion has located him for her very own. What a riot!"

"Well, just what do you mean by that?" Marion asked suspiciously.

But Mrs. Fox broke in: "Oh, dearie! Are you really going to marry him—"

"And give nuggets for bridal favors?" Beach suggested.

"Yeah, just what are you going to do with him, Marion?" Fox wanted to know. "As far as I can make out he comes under the head of 'Interesting, if True.' Why all the clamor?"

"What am I going to do with him?" Marion echoed. "I don't know—haven't made up my mind. Except one thing, I am not going to marry him—"

"Then," said Sapley earnestly, "the first shooting show girl that gets her eyes on him will. And what do you get out of that? How about all this jack he's got—"

"I wouldn't marry that hick if he had all the sealskins in the world!" Marion declared with sudden spirit. "The Eskimo's bride? Not for Marion!"

"H-m!" Beach smiled shrewdly. "Something interesting happened before we got to that island."

The girl colored in spite of her supreme self-possession. But she joined the general laugh readily enough. "Oh, he's a self-starter, if that's what you mean. And the stone hatchet method ought to make a hit with most women, but— No, I don't know just yet what I'll do with him, but I'd like to take him back to Broadway. Maybe I will."

"What for? You say that you don't want his sealskin millions."

"What for? What for? Can't any of you see that this big hick from Kalvik Island would be the biggest thrill that's been handed New York since Barnum found the Cardiff giant? Imagine it! The Northern Lights Kid coming down the big trail shedding sealskins and walrus tusks, tipping bellboys and waiters with gold nuggets, dining off a hundred dollars' worth of fricasseed blubber every day, pockets stuffed full of smoked salmon and silver-fox furs, wearing one of these Eskimo fancy dress ball costumes—"

"Maybe with a string of malamute dogs!" Sapley chimed in.

"And completely surrounded by ladies from the Midnight Roof!" Field chuckled.

"Talk about millionaire miners! Talk about Scotty of Death Valley, and all these other high-rolling spenders from the bushes!" Marion exclaimed. "This one would make them all look like cripples selling shoestrings. Publicity! Rightly handled, I can see whole volumes of it."

"All right," Fox agreed. "All right—all right! I grant you all that. I give you right. Publicity, yes—but what the hell are you selling? Soap?"

"Yeah, Marion, what's your game?" Sapley echoed wisely.

"Don't you think it would be so much nicer just to marry him?" Mrs. Fox urged.

Marion answered the last question first. "No, I don't. As to what I'm selling—well, I'm not quite sure, but I had sort of an idea, and I was going to give it to Douglas, when we can talk it over in private. If it's worth something, it might make up for losing the launch."

Beach rose. "I call that rather a pointed hint," he said lazily. "Come on, Al, we've got to look over those guns—"

"And I want to throw on some rags for dinner," Mrs. Fox said.

"Yes," Marion cried, "you all do. Whatever you do, dress—dress the limit. Remember this is Stonehatchet's first party, and we've got to do it right. I'm depending on making an impression."

"Good Lord!" Sapley groaned. "Soup and fish, I suppose, and I was promised I wouldn't have to chafe my neck on a stiff collar the whole two months."

"But you'll do it—for me, Al?"

"Sure. I'll die for you, sweetie, whenever you say!"

Marion was left alone with Douglas Fox. "Now," Fox said abruptly, "you've got some kind of business idea, eh? I can see you have."

"Well—you said if you ran across any good chances up here you'd take them. You said things had been quiet—"

"Too quiet, since the last oil field flivved," Fox admitted gloomily.

"Then, why not sealskins?" said Marion.

"Sealskins? What do you mean by that? I haven't any sealskins. Do you expect me to murder this Stonehatchet man and steal his—or what?"

She wrinkled her forehead and her brown eyes became dreamy with speculation. "Douglas, I don't just know. But there must be some connection between this man Hayes's cave full of prime sealskins—and the wonderful chance to exploit him in the big town. Somewhere in that combination there's coin. I can smell it. I'd like to see you get it."

"I might change my name and open a fur store on Sixth Avenue," Fox suggested with heavy sarcasm. "But without any kidding, if there's money there I don't see it. If this bird's got so many sealskins it would take a ship and a regular expedition to carry them away. And anyway they belong to him. I don't see—"

"How about a stock company—and a regular outfit to bring the skins to market?"

"Well, what's the use, providing he could be kidded into giving me a piece of the velvet in it?"

"He could be kidded," Marion promised. "He could be kidded into anything."

"Nope, Marion, I don't see money there. As a matter of fact, there isn't so much in sealskins, anyway. The price has been dropping, even with a restricted market."

"How many people know that?" Marion cried. "Why, sealskins, to the regular everyday garden variety of sucker, are like diamonds. You'd think so if you tried to buy a coat for Ada."

"I did," Fox admitted with a wry face.

"There, you see! And that's all the average man does know about them. Look here, Douglas, suppose that our Mr. Stonehatchet was to burst on Broadway like an aurora borealis some fine night, and create the kind of sensation he could make if he was handled by an expert like me? Suppose he bloomed out in all the papers, and showed in theaters and roofs and hotels, shedding gold nuggets, and the whole United States of suckers learned he owned a mountain of sealskins and was going to send a ship to his desert island to bring in a load—and they could buy stock in the expedition for a limited time only at the ridiculous sum of a dime, the tenth part of a dollar, per each share—or something like that. Would you sell any stock?"

Fox's light blue eyes began to shine. "Now I get you! You said something. Sucker bait—I never thought of that!"

Marion laughed and confessed: "I never did, either, till we got to talking—and it sort of worked itself out. But I can see it now. It looks to me, if it was properly handled, as if you'd find our friend Jonathan Hayes of Kalvik as good as any of your dry oil wells."

"And you'll handle him? It couldn't be done without you, Marion."

"It won't be done without me!" Marion laughed. "And you'll find me expensive, too."

"Whoosh!" Fox exploded derisively. "Write your own ticket. You're worth whatever you ask in this. And I'll talk to him tonight. Oil wells! This bird ought to be worth a whole field of big gushers! Only thing is, will he do it?" Marion rose and smiled down on him, a shadowy, mysterious smile.

"Will he do it? Not for you, Douglas, though of course you'll have to put the proposition to him first. But he will do it if I tell him to."

Fox grinned admiringly. "I'll bet he'll do any trick you tell him to. You're a dangerous girl. But, honest, Marion, why don't you marry this fellow if he's worth all that, and keep the money in the family? I'll resign my claim. You don't owe me a cent. Go on—grab a stake for yourself!" Marion shook her head, and the mane of old-gold hair flew out about her slender shoulders.

"Nope—no wedding bells. What I get from Jonathan Stone-hatchet Hayes of Kalvik Island I'll take in your way—strictly business. I'm set on that."

"You're the boss," Fox murmured. "If you say so, that goes. I'll sound him out tonight—and you promise to put him over the hurdles if I say the word?"

"I'll deliver him, postage paid, whenever you say," Marion promised earnestly. With her shadowy smile she was gone.

CHAPTER VIII

OVER THE HURDLES

MARION READE WENT to her comfortable stateroom direct from her interview with Fox. She got out a party frock, the one best calculated to astonish Jonathan Hayes, and laid plans for the evening toilet. Ada Fox had confided as she had entered the little corridor between their rooms that she was going to wedge all of her hundred and sixty-nine pounds into that gold cloth thing she had bought when there was a Turkish bath handy to keep her down to ringside weight.

Marion encouraged her. She hoped they would all lay themselves out to give Mr. Stonehatchet an idea of what he had been missing all these years.

Of her own frock Marion had no doubts at all. It was an old thing, of course, just something carried along for an emergency party during the two months' cruise, but she knew in her bones it would give the man from Kalvik a thrill. She looked up from the handful of silk and gilt tissue she had unpacked, glancing out of the port toward the bare rocks and windbitten hills of Kalvik seen under a gray and lowering sky.

"Mr. Man," she said, addressing the landscape, "I've undertaken to do a lot to you. I wonder if I'm going to deliver the goods as easily as I think I am?"

She had promised Douglas Fox she would put her pet wild man over the hurdles when he said the word. She had contracted to bring him to Broadway like a dancing bear—and as yet Jonathan Hayes was scarcely consulted; in fact had declared his firm intention of staying forever on Kalvik Island.

"It would be ghastly if he should balk, after all I boasted to Fox!" Marion thought.

But she did not believe Hayes would balk. She had supreme confidence in her ability to get her own way, born of considerable experience.

She hadn't forgotten what Hayes called her in that emotional moment when he spoke what was nearest his heart. "A tinsel woman," was she? "Utterly, damnably useless!" She frowned at the thought of the humiliations he had heaped on her, his praises for the Aleut, his patent scorn of her conduct in the defense of the ranch-house, and finally that outburst that confessed his judgment of her—and his weakness at the same time.

Mr. Jonathan Stonehatchet Hayes would find that a tinsel woman could be a very dangerous sort before they parted. He dared to kiss her—and scorn her in the same breath as if that kiss confessed a shameful weakness. She got hot all over when she thought of that. It made her hate him and vow to pay him back. That had prompted her cold-blooded bargain with Fox.

Not that she could hurt Hayes financially. She knew money would mean nothing to this man. But once she got him to New York, to Broadway, on her own ground, she would find ways to make him suffer. The business proposition suggested to Fox would be the means to that end.

Hayes confessed he was mad about her. She triumphed in that confession. That gave her the power she sought. During her long and intricate process of self-beautification Marion considered these matters.

The little toilet table, her familiar surroundings of comfort and luxury, made the weird events of the night on Kalvik Island appear in a very different light. They vastly magnified the importance of Marion Reade, and made revenge on Hayes appear in the light of right and reason.

Also, aside from these motives, her professional instinct prompted her. She could appreciate the wonderful theatricalism of Jonathan Hayes of Kalvik invading the bright-light district that furnishes New York with its sensational reading. All the showman blood in her cried aloud to stage this drama.

Before the tender had landed the party from the yacht Hayes had followed Marion to the beach. He came abjectly, trying to stammer proper apologies for his rudeness. Marion forgave him without melting her displeasure one degree. She had the satisfaction of knowing that he still suffered remorse when she gave him his invitation to join the company aboard at dinner, and went back to the yacht. He would come, and he would come groveling.

Dressed finally, and fully aware that the dull bronze of her gown made wonderful effects of her dull gold hair and creamy bare neck and shoulders, she quit her stateroom, humming a gay little tune. In the corridor she encountered Beach. The sportsman stopped her, a hand on her arm.

"Marion! I didn't get a chance to tell you before how glad— how deeply thankful I was when I knew you were safe. If you knew the hell I went through when you were missed—while we didn't know but you had drowned at sea! Then to see you there on the island, safe, knowing what you had been through— Marion, I tell you a fellow realizes then what a girl like you means in his life!"

Marion answered composedly: "I'm glad if you missed me. It's nice to be missed. I'm almost glad you—suffered." She eyed Beach a little narrowly, wondering, if he had taken a cocktail too many.

Mightier huntresses than Marion had aimed their darts at Irving Beach. The man had the name of a family firmly established in Manhattan society. Though he didn't play that game much, he was always eligible. He had an income, too, enough to own a small yacht and spend most of his time big game hunting. When he didn't hunt he lived on Manhattan, in a small but desirable apartment hotel, and was seen at first nights, at races, at roofs and even, rarely, at the opera. He was reputed to have had many affairs with women, and to be too thoroughly sophisticated ever to tangle himself or his money.

Marion, who had the modern young woman's habit of considering all men dispassionately in relation to her own ambitions, had left her decision on Beach unpronounced. This cruise had given her opportunities to further an acquaintance heretofore casual. Sometimes she considered what she might be able to do with his money and name—but Beach had proved a wily fish. And after all, she wasn't sure she wanted to land him. He might be embarrassingly hard to handle.

His sudden vehemence now surprised her.

"I don't suppose you wasted one thought on me—when you were drowning in the surf—or these rascals were trying to kill you!"

"Yes, I did," she answered frankly. "I thought about you all. A vision of Al Sapley's shining bald head is the clearest thing I remember."

"You know that isn't what I mean—That's a wonderful dress, my dear. I wonder if you really know what a little beauty you are in that yellow stuff?"

"Do you suppose I'd dress like this for the blind man's ball, my dear chap? We aim to please."

"Do you! I wonder—" Beach stooped and brushed her lips with his, swiftly and deftly, before she could step away. He did not try to hold her when she did step back, but stood smiling frankly at her, in the dimly lit little corridor. "Do you always aim to please—really?" he asked huskily.

Marion had not turned a hair. She said composedly now, "I thought you had had one too many. No really first class hunter gets fuddled on cocktails—does he? Now run along and dress your prettiest. Remember I'm counting on your shining tonight."

A sailor, who had been posted on watch, brought word from the deck that the guest of the evening had put out from Kalvik

Island in a native skin boat. The news electrified the five who had been waiting in the saloon of the *Frivolity*.

Marion snatched up a glittering wrap and wound it about her slender shoulders, preparatory to going to the deck to greet Jonathan Hayes.

"Remember," she cautioned them half in mockery and part in earnest, "you're dealing with a cave man, but he's not an idiot. Whatever you do, don't laugh—and don't startle him too much. I don't guarantee that he won't break dishes and maybe bend silver knives between his fingers. He may insist on bringing his own salmon along and eating it alive, and wriggling, but, girls and boys, he's our little guest, and let's treat him as such."

"Bring on His Grace the Duke of Malamute," Al Sapley cackled. "Never mind all that chatter."

Marion disappeared in the companion-way, and they exchanged an interested and complacent glance. The three men had dressed with all the formalities of dinner jacket and immaculate linen; Mrs. Fox had squirmed into the outgrown décolleté, and what of her was not encased bulged forth exuberantly.

The table was set with six places. The electroliers in the beamed ceiling glowed through pearl glass. Their light was reflected from the yacht's silver service and cut-glass. The room was at its best at this gala hour of the day, its rich wood paneling and tapestries glowing with soft colors. The white jacketed Japanese came and went on little errands concerning the table, velvet footed. The saloon and the four elaborately dressed people in it promised to be a striking contrast to Marion Reade's newest discovery, the ice-age man.

They heard Marion's voice and then their guest arrived. Jonathan Hayes, also, had dressed for dinner. He loomed enormous in the door, clad in hooded parka of reindeer hide, his face framed in a sunburst of fox fur that lined the hood. The garment had been embroidered elaborately in the Indian manner with beads and bits of red and green flannel, and even tiny ivory gew-gaws. Embroidered likewise were the fancy fur topped mukluks on his feet. Under his arm the man clasped a bundle of sealskins. For the moment that he paused in that door, towering over them, barbaric, huge, a man of dignity and power, he fulfilled every anticipation. The four spectators were conscious of a thrill from this promise of much drama.

And for the moment, Marion, ridiculously dwarfed by Hayes's side, had the radiant complacence of the successful showman. "Ladies and gentlemen," she announced demurely, "Mr. Jonathan Hayes of Kalvik Island." Then followed the personal presentations.

Consciously the moment had been chosen, the actors dressed and the stage set to impress the primitive mind of Jonathan Hayes. None of them was certain as to just what they expected of the man when first he was confronted with civilization, but each expected a demonstration. There was enough to the picture at least to surprise almost any man out of touch with life for a few years—the elaborate comfort of the yacht, the formal dress of the men, Mrs. Fox more than amply filling a very daring gown, and Marion revealed, as she laid aside her wrap, with bare shoulders and breast, a slender little shining bronze figure with much exposed stockings of bronze silk, and bronze slippers on her feet. But there was no demonstration by Jonathan Hayes.

Al Sapley's "Duke of Malamute" bowed formally to Ada Fox and accepted her exuberant fleshiness as he might the manifestations of one of his own Aleutian volcanos—a startling event, but in the course of nature. The hands of the men he grasped hard. The room itself he surveyed with a long, frank, pleased glance and declared himself at once, "Mr. Fox, I never thought anything could be so beautiful as your ship."

Fox beamed with an owner's pride. Sapley cried tolerantly, "Oh, she's fair enough—a fair enough little garbage scow!" But Fox whirled on him. "She's a damn sight better than the Iron Steamboat to Coney, and that's the best you ever saw before!" Even Hayes joined the laugh at Sapley's expense; and when he laughed with them the tension was gone. They all felt that a party had begun, but one in which their guest in some way, almost at once, ceased to be a stranger.

After dinner, a prolonged meal enlivened with Fox's own private stock of wines for all but the guest, who drank nothing, Hayes was escorted on a thorough tour of the boat that included the wonders of its little wireless which was sending news of the raid on Kalvik Island to distant revenue cutters; the perfection of a compact engine room, a refrigerating plant, an electric plant, bridge telegraphs, and a searchlight.

Sapley fell behind with Irving Beach.

"Say!" he whined confidentially, "that bird's been kidding our Marion. If he's a stonehatchet I'm living back with the big lizards! Talk about stage presence! Did you watch him at dinner? Why if I was to see him eating pie with a knife I'd know that was the latest thing in swell society and do it myself!"

"He's no fool, that's all," Beach answered. "Any savage chief that never saw our civilization can throw a bluff like that—and they most always do. The reason is, he looks at these non-essentials for what they are. He doesn't let little things get magnified out of their own importance. He thinks for himself—as a man should, but usually doesn't."

"He's a real he-man all right," Sapley sighed. "I'll say he is—and you can take my tip on it, old chap, Marion isn't going to make a monkey out of him without working a lot harder than she ever did before in her life!"

Beach answered thoughtfully, "Then don't bet any money on your hunch. That girl can come nearer getting what she wants than any I ever saw—and I've seen a lot!"

Marion and Irving Beach found themselves alone in the yacht's saloon, set as a lounge now, its tables folded back and all traces of dinner service gone.

Fox and Jonathan Hayes were closeted in the businesslike coziness of the pilot house where the promoter was talking business to his guest. Ada Fox had confided with her usual frankness, "I've got to beat it to my stateroom, dearie, and take a can opener to this dress before I bust it wide open! You can excuse me to your cave man." Al Sapley had slipped away at a significant glance from Beach.

Beach moved restlessly, eying the girl with open admiration. Marion's bare shoulders were strangely square and boyish, and the round, slender column of her neck rose in a fascinating right angle to their squareness. The short-cut gold hair became her small head and heightened the charming suggestion of perfect immaturity. Beach was beginning to see all these perfections with an interest that made them quite new to him.

"Look here, Marion," he said uneasily. "What's your game with this Hayes fellow?"

"I've about decided to take him back to Broadway—on a leash—"

"Why?"

"Oh, business—"

"Fox in it?"

"Yep."

"Humph!"

Irving Beach never commented on the business morals of his host. He was too much a gentleman. But it did not need much insight to read his mind. Marion read it in his grunt and his glance, and her own unspoken thoughts peeped out of her eyes and agreed with his without explanation or apology for her part in the game.

"But is just—business—your interest?"

"Isn't that rather personal?"

"If it is it's because I have a right—the way you make me feel—"

"Please! Save things like that for morning. We're all so much more—normal—in the mornings. I could tell if you meant it then—"

"I do mean it!" Beach rose, bending over her, his firm, white hands gripping the arm of her chair. "And you know I mean it," he added. "Does it mean anything to you?"

She made a face of perplexity and protest. "How should I know! I've got one cave man on my hands already. Must you start now?"

"Ditch your cave man, Marion. I—"

"And lose a profit? Say—"

"I can show you better profits than that—and I'll let in Fox, if you feel obligated there—"

"I'll go through with Mr. Stonehatchet, first—"

"Then he does mean more to you than business!"

"Sweet lady! I don't deny it. He's amusing. When I get him to Broadway I'm going to have a lot of fun with the Duke of Malamute. Fun—and profit—"

"Look out it doesn't end at the Little Church Around the Corner and you wearing a bridal veil of sealskins!"

"I'll tell you something for your own satisfaction," Marion said coldly. "Wherever it ends, it won't end with me in the arms of Mr. Jonathan Hayes. I know what I want of him, and it's not—that. That ought to satisfy you for one evening." Beach caught the flash of her brown eye and the ring of her words. He already knew her for no fool. She had maneuvered a frail bark among many shoals since first he had heard of her, and she had got what she wanted without compromise. Before he had felt any keen personal regard he had conceived a high admiration for the girl's ingenuity and courage.

But he insisted still, "Then when you're done with Hayes—when you have shown him off to your heart's delight, and astonished Broadway and got all the publicity you and Fox need for whatever scheme you have in mind—when you've shown your prize, and the tinsel has worn off him, will you promise to listen to something serious?" Marion started to say, "I never promise," when Fox entered the saloon.

Fox made a gesture of helplessness. "What's the good of

arguing with a man who isn't interested at all in money? You haven't anything to convince him with!"

"But you're satisfied he has the skins—enough to make it worthwhile?" Marion asked.

"Oh, he's got them. And it wouldn't break the bank to send a ship after them—if he could be persuaded to tell where they are. But—well, you promised him delivered, postage paid. I leave it to you!"

"You'll go through? You're satisfied it's worth doing?"

"Deliver your wild man, and I'll do the rest," Fox promised.

Marion's eyes snapped. "All right. Send him down to me."

"Done in a minute!" Fox paused at the door. "How about you, Beach? Marion will probably want to do her man taming uninterrupted. Join me and Al and the captain for a game of poker?"

"Be along in just a minute," Beach promised, lingering.

"I don't want you here," Marion said coldly. "You'll ruin the scene."

Beach hesitated, nervously touching one article and another of the room's furnishings.

"You didn't answer my question," he suggested. "Will you promise to listen to me—"

Marion rose and approached him, taking him by his coat lapels. "Beach, be a good sport! Go, before Hayes comes here!"

"And your promise?"

"I'll promise anything—to get rid of you!"

Beach touched her hair lightly with his lips. He caught her hands in his and held them. "You wonder!" he exclaimed.

They were aware simultaneously that Hayes stood in the door. He stared and flushed slowly. "I—I didn't understand. Perhaps I had better go—"

Marion laughed lightly. "It's all right. Come in. Mr. Beach has promised to let us have a farewell chat together. Fox tells me you're not going to accept his aid."

Beach nodded an excuse and left them.

"Sit down," Marion invited, seating herself and dragging another chair close to face her.

Jonathan Hayes continued to stand, ignoring her and the invitation. She bore this for several uneasy moments, then tried again, saying softly; "So you've really decided not to go. We say good-by—tonight?"

Hayes said coolly: "I told you this afternoon why I'm not interested in your world. Can you show me a good reason to change my mind?"

Marion sighed. "If I told the truth—and said the only darn reason I know of is because it would tickle me pink to have you go, that wouldn't be any argument. It would only sound silly, wouldn't it?"

"How could it possibly please you?"

"Well, I don't know. Somehow I wanted to see you do it, that's all. I'd set my heart on showing you the sights. I—You saved my life, you see; it struck me as a fine idea to pay you back by showing you what living really is; to show you how to get the money that's coming to you, and get some fun out of it after you've got hold of it. I—call it just a fool delight in butting into another person's business, if you like, but I had set my heart on taking you by the hand and showing you all the jolly old world that is yours to play with if you want it." She lowered her eyes; there was an artistic trace of moisture about them when she timidly looked up again.

Hayes stared mightily. "You! You really wanted me to go— you want to do things like that for me?"

"Yes. Why not?"

He waded slowly in his bewilderment.

"I can't understand—that you should be interested—and yet you love this other man—"

"What other man?"

"Beach. I saw you in his arms. He kissed you."

Marion burst out laughing, that tinkling, musical laugh that fascinated him by its delicacy even while it left him more bewildered. "Oh, Beach! That kiss—"

"I didn't see you fight against that kiss. You must love him—

Her dancing eyes and brilliant smile, the shrug of her square, boyish shoulders made light of that. "You poor baby!" she exclaimed, commiserating. "What a lot you have got to learn about women—and kisses!"

"Then you don't love him? You're not promised to him—"

"Poof! That was Damon and Pythias—Haig and Haig—brother and sister. I think Beach is a dear—but I couldn't sue him for breach of promise just because he got silly and kissed me. Don't judge me by the men who kiss me!"

He began accusingly, almost angry: "I kissed you this afternoon—because—well, because just the sight of you—your nearness—your beauty made me do it. You hated that. You hate me for it now—though you say you forgive me and accept my gift of atonement."

In spite of her firm intention she forgot herself to answer tartly: "I'm not used to being mangled by a steam roller—nor classed in the same breath with a painted woman of the gutter." But she amended with the suggestion: "And perhaps I was a little afraid—of what your kiss—might mean. There are men—whose kisses—a girl might be scared of."

Hayes strode to her chair and stood looking down on her, dwarfing her, challenging her gaze with his steady, dark eyes. "I kissed you because I love you. You know it. I apologize for frightening you, but not for loving you."

"It strikes me," Marion said hurriedly, "that this is a long way from the topic of the evening. What has this to do with your joining Fox, who has made you a very generous offer, and coming with us to New York?"

"It has everything to do. You know that. You know that you are the one reason that will take me to New York—or to hell, if you want it so. Admit that you know it."

"I don't admit anything."

"You know that is true."

"I'll accept your word for it, then—if that pleases you."

Hayes nodded. "Listen, then," he said slowly, his face serious, the black eyes burning, "I'll go to Broadway—I'll go anywhere—for your promise in exchange."

"What promise?"

"Just this: that you'll give me the chance to prove my love. You must give me the chance to prove myself, against your civilization. I'm not afraid of it. And when I win, when I know your world as you know it, so that there is equality between us, I shall ask you to be my wife—Until then you promise to wait for me?" She heard his proposal, and the scheming mind of her registered astonishment that he had asked so little. This was a simple promise indeed, less than she had expected to promise. But at the same time emotion warned her that the man was serious—and his seriousness frightened her with thoughts of what might happen later. He would be the man to hold her to any promise made—and hard to answer when she had to answer him finally. The recklessness that carried her through plenty of tight places whispered now: "What of it? New York's a long way from Kalvik—and you boasted that this Stonehatchet was your meat. Let's go!"

"I will promise you that," she said. There was no demonstration, and that was even more startling to her than his savage embrace of the afternoon.

Hayes nodded satisfaction.

"Then, I'll say good night," he said with strange and characteristic lack of concern. "Tell Fox I'll talk with him in the morning about arrangements."

He nodded and turned toward the door. Astonished, she watched him go. She ventured with a little giggle at a parting shot: "But wait till you've seen Broadway and the girlies there. You'll be asking me to give you back your promise."

At the door Hayes retorted sternly:

"You're a queer lot, all of you, talking drivel instead of ideas. And that's the most idiotic remark of all! Good night."

He was gone.

Marion Reade, who had hated him for his savage embrace, was even more shocked now that he had ignored a patent opportunity to kiss her again. She found she hated him even more for that.

CHAPTER IX

THE SUCKER BAIT

THE *FRIVOLITY* WAS bound south, with Kalvik Island long sunk below the horizon and dimming a little even in the memory of Jonathan Hayes. Seas were smooth and the sun still shone the better part of the twenty-four hours, though with every mile of southing they would draw away from midnight sunsets that were followed at once by sunrises, so that night existed merely as a technicality.

Jonathan Hayes was much on deck. The first day or so his glances all had been astern, toward the island that for twenty-seven years was his world. He had seen Kalvik dwindle and fade off the horizon with the look of a man who knew that much would happen and many things change before he saw it again—and he continued to look back, acknowledging the ties of a lifetime association.

Then his interest was transferred to the world that lay ahead, and he stared for hours beyond the bow of the yacht, grave and silent.

Beach, who watched him often, remarked several times to his companions: "Reminds me somehow of when I was about seven and they shipped me off to a school. I'd never been anywhere; kept close at home. I'll never forget that funny, lost, awful feeling—I suppose Columbus felt that way, too. There's a lot of thinking going on in that chap's head; he's feeling a lot, too, but you'd never guess it from his poker face."

"Well, you got to hand it to him—he's got something to

think *with!*" Al Sapley maintained loyally. "That's more than a lot of men in his fix have got."

Strange, that of them all it was Sapley who was always first to defend their stonehatchet man. The queer, bald-headed wise-cracker had conceived an enormous admiration for what he called the front, or stage presence of Jonathan Hayes. He and Hayes talked often and long, and Al discoursed always of the world that he knew for the benefit of the man from another world.

"You don't need to worry, sucker!" Al would maintain en-couragingly. "You've got the one thing a man has to have to beat this Broadway game—that's nerve. And that's all there is to the whole show—bluffing! Believe you me, there's more hicks at Broadway and Forty-Second Street than any other one place in the world. I don't mean just the ones that hurts their eyes watching the electric signs, either. I know what I'm talking about, because I've sold 'em gold bricks and oil-well stock and Kickapoo Indian Sagawa from Hell to Halifax. There was an old bird that said one time, 'The bigger they are, the harder they fall,' and that's about the wisest crack ever was made. Go after 'em, kid! Eat 'em up!"

To advice like this Jonathan Hayes would listen gravely, puzzling over Al's strange words, asking enlightenment from time to time, smiling in perfect accord with Al's humorous views of life.

"He's a most amusing and likable companion," Hayes con-fided to Marion, "and his talk prepares me for what to expect of your bright lights."

Marion went privately to Al. "A little of the soft pedal on your advice, please, Al," she said. "We don't want our cave man too sophisticated before he gets to Broadway. That would spoil the whole show!"

"I get you," Al grinned. "What you and Fox want is a Simon-pure sucker, without benzoate of soda or other adulterants. Otherwise you're afraid he might know too much—"

"It's your meal ticket as well as mine," Marion reminded him.

"Sure! But I'm telling you and Fox, too, you've got this bird all wrong. He ain't a dumb-bell and no amount of gilding can make him one. He was born wise!"

Marion lounged in a deck-chair on an afternoon of pale golden sunshine. Sitka had been promised before evening of the next day at the latest. Fine weather had made the *Frivolity's* run unusually good. Everybody was in splendid humor and excited with the nearness of the first point of civilization the yacht would touch. Beach, who sat beside her, was saying: "If it gives people like us a little thrill to come back to paved streets and electric lights and shops after a few weeks' absence, think what it means to our distinguished guest! And, Marion, I'm going to remind you again that you made me a promise the night that chap Hayes came aboard—"

"Promise?" Marion wrinkled her brows. "I don't remember making any promises—"

"And I'm quite sure you do," Beach said positively. "You promised me when you were through exploiting this cave man of yours you would listen to something serious—"

"Oh, then! But I'm not done—or haven't even begun, for that matter!"

"Just the same, I don't mean to let you forget. Did it ever occur to you to figure just what you're getting out of this publicity business of yours?"

"A darn good living," Marion said promptly.

"Exactly. A meal ticket. That's all. If you were an actress or a singer—if there was a career in it—"

"There is a career. It's a game, and I like it. And I'm going to be the world's greatest press-agent before I get through—"

"What does that amount to?"

"It amounts to independence. That's what most women like—if they'd be honest about it. I don't have to give a hang any more about any man—"

"You're wrong, my dear, and you know it. You do depend on

men, depend on them all the time. You depend upon impressing them with your charm in order to get your various schemes over. You depend upon your skill that makes them think you might be dangerously interested in them; and your cold-blooded judgment that keeps them always at a distance—"

Marion drew herself up indignantly. "Well, I must say—"

"Hold on! I'm not saying anything disparaging, nor thinking it. It's a woman's game, played harder than ever now that women are competing everywhere in a man's world, but it's a dangerous game. To play it a girl must be sure she has a heart of stone. Did you ever think of the danger if some day you might care for a man—and cease to pretend?"

"That's consistent, coming from you!" she mocked, half angry. "And you have just reminded me I promised to let you try to make me care for you some time. You warn me of dangers!"

"No," Beach said soberly, "I want to show you that your safety lies in caring for one man—and the right one. If you really have a heart—oh, I've watched you for two years now! I've watched your game and applauded it, and admired your skill and wondered all the time if you had the capacity to care for any man—"

Beach stopped abruptly. "Hello. Come, sit down," he invited over his shoulder.

Hayes, who had strolled toward them, nodded and took the chair Beach left vacant. Hayes looked stonily toward the horizon and answered Marion's conversation briefly. "Why all this gloom?" she demanded.

Hayes turned on her. "You're a funny lot, all of you," he burst out. "And you in particular—"

"I don't know that that's flattering."

"It isn't. Do you ever mean what you say—and do? If so, when do you mean it?"

"Good Heaven, what—"

"What kind of women are you? Is your civilization made up of women like you? You, for instance! I kissed you and you hated me. Beach kissed you and you laughed and said it was brother and sister. You said you forgave me, and you make me think you might be made to care. You say Beach is nothing to you, yet you prefer his company. And from what you say and the way you act, you might be in love with every man on this ship. Is this a mad world you're taking me into?"

Marion laughed. "You're jealous," she taunted.

"I think I am, indeed!"

"Hayes, learn to discount all you see and hear. Believe only what you find out for yourself."

"I know this! You play a silly game. Be careful it isn't a dangerous one!"

"I play the one game I know—the one game that a girl without money or backing, without any particular education or equipment who is ambitious to get on can play in my world!" Marion said vehemently. First Beach, then Hayes, both with this warning! She felt the necessity of justifying herself.

"Consider a minute what I've been up against since I've been old enough to find out I was entitled to some happiness out of life, and made up my mind to collect it. We lived in a shabby little house in a shabby little manufacturing town. My father worked at a lathe and earned barely enough to keep us going. My oldest brother and sister worked in mills. There was little beauty in that town; none where we lived. The yard about our shabby, bare, unpainted house was cinders and mud. There, and in cobblestone streets black and greasy, I grew up. I was fed up with that before I was old enough to put aside dolls. My mother was faded, shrill-voiced, breaking down. My father was broken in spirit. He didn't know just what it was all about, but he knew things were all wrong. 'Not for Marion!' I said, and I meant it.

"Give me credit, I had more sense than the others. I had sense enough to know that schooling counted and I studied and read everything I could get hold of. When I started work I was a cash girl in a dry goods store. I took my first savings to get to a small city, where I worked in a bigger and smarter store, and watched our customers and learned what to wear and how to talk and act. And there I learned that the man with the softest job of all was the man who wrote the store's advertising. Do you know what I did with my spare time? I practiced writing advertising!

"I took the stuff I wrote to the store's advertising man, up to his house, after hours. He was bald-headed, married, loaded to the eyes with debts and babies and troubles, but I kidded him into helping me, into teaching me. I looked so forlorn and innocent he had to sympathize.

"When I thought I knew all I could get I went to a man I'd heard of who was starting a mail order business. I put on all my best clothes and threw an awful bluff and got a job out of it—on the strength of my good looks. I never fooled myself about that. But I made good on that job, made good so well that even that pinhead saw he didn't dare go too far with me. He learned to treat me like any other man he hired.

"From there it was a jump to the big town—New York. And I began all over again, dressing like a million dollars when I didn't have even half enough to eat, and smiling and flirting and kidding men into giving me my chance. When I got that chance I made good again. I climbed over men to do it, and never a man of the lot that ever got beyond the privilege of staking me to a free meal now and then. If they ever expected more they were fools—that's all." Marion's eyes flashed.

"It was sink or swim for me. A fight for life. And all I had to fight with was good looks—and nerve. I fought!"

"You did all this alone—without help?" Hayes exclaimed.

"Without anybody to help me—or pay the bills—or get me introductions—or anything. Not that I wasn't offered help, but those offers came from men; there was a price-tag on every offer. The price was much too high to suit me. So I kept on bluffing and scheming and smiling until my lips were ready to crack—and I got on, Hayes. You'll see, I got on well!"

To Jonathan Hayes she looked very small—very much like a child—and astonishingly lovely sitting straight, animated by her recital, the wind stirring her short-cut hair of old gold. And yet how old she was in wisdom, prematurely old!

He saw Marion in a new guise, fighting single-handed against a man's world, spurred to great ambitions. He saw her as some small and weaker animal in a jungle, surviving not by fang and claw, but by cunning, which is the weaker animal's only defense against the powerful ones that prey. In such a fight to exist there is no choice of weapons. The girl accepted life's challenge and triumphed by the only means she had.

Hayes exclaimed: "That's bravery! I understand now—and thank you. Thank you for letting me understand. If you knew how different this makes things seem—how I honor—and admire—your courage!"

He was on his feet as he said it and he bowed before her as one soldier saluting the proved courage of another.

"You are very wonderful!" he added, and walked away hurriedly.

For once Marion Reade was thoroughly astonished. It was not improbable that she had thought these things of herself—and she had been praised before, but life had taught her to discount words of commendation and look for the motive behind them.

There was no self-seeking motive behind Hayes's words. With disconcerting simplicity he said what he meant.

She flushed with delight and a lump came into her throat. Her eyes were damp.

Beach came upon Fox in the saloon, deep in calculations. "Come in," Fox hailed him jovially. "Just figuring out our plan of campaign. Boy, she's a cat!"

"Campaign? You mean—"

"I mean this fellow Hayes and his first appearance in big time. Listen! We're going to give New York a thrill!"

"What's the idea—if it's any of my business?"

"No secrets from you," Fox said heartily. "I'm going to promote a little company to get all these sealskins Hayes knows about. And the start of it will be the neatest piece of advertising the town has seen in years. Look, one fine day, all by himself, this big boob from the northern lights blows into the bright lights belt, all togged out like an Eskimo. Registers at a Broadway hotel. Hands the bell-hops little gold nuggets for tips. Maybe gives the room clerk a sealskin. Wanders out by himself and takes a slant at the big buildings, munching a smoked salmon as he goes. What will the reporters say when they hear of that?"

"They'll say it's a plant—ask what show he's advertising," Beach answered promptly.

"Right," Fox agreed. "Just what all the wise birds will say *until they talk to Jonathan Hayes.* Do you get the difference now?"

"I think I do. You mean that the man's queer honesty—his sincerity—"

"Yeah! Why? Because Hayes *believes* all this stuff. It's everyday truth to him. And you can't talk to him without feeling that way about it yourself. Why, he's got even me kidded—when I'm with him. And then, when he springs the story of his sealskins and how he's come to the big town to fit out a ship and go get them! When he tells about that battle on the island, with Marion Reade the yellow-haired heroine! Oh, boy!"

"Perhaps you're right, Fox—I believe you are. Hayes has the sort of honesty that will put it over, properly handled. And the inevitable result, I suppose, will be the formation of a company to help him out by that eminent philanthropic capitalist Douglas Fox? That, and the sale of stock?"

"Something like that," Fox grinned. "See this list? That's a lot of props I've got to lay in at Sitka: Indian baskets, ivory junk, little gold nuggets and scenery like that for our Eskimo millionaire."

Beach smiled ironically. "There's one thing," he suggested. "What about this other chap—this Captain Darius Cook? He seems to be rather a resourceful lot himself, judging by what happened on the island. If Cook isn't picked up by the revenue men, which is very unlikely, isn't he going to hear about this, after all the publicity, and maybe beat you to the sealskins?"

Fox shrugged his heavy shoulders. "He might—if he can find out just where they are," he admitted.

"This news will encourage him to look pretty thoroughly."

"Yes—I suppose it will."

"The value of the skins naturally will be magnified in newspaper accounts. Cook may beat you to it."

Fox smiled wisely. "Beach, just between you and me, do you believe this yarn about sealskins?"

"Why not? Hayes does—" '

"Oh, Hayes! He's just a dumb-bell!"

"Cook does. He's no dumb-bell evidently."

"No, he's a roughneck—by all accounts. Just a lowbrow with a gaspipe. But do you, a fellow like me, who knows his way about, believe any fortune in sealskins is going to stick around in some ridiculous ice cave all these years—and nobody help himself? I don't!"

"Evidently," Beach said thoughtfully, "you're not figuring on taking a profit out of the pelts."

"I'm not. I'm going to clean up by selling the stock. Of course, in time, to show good faith, we'll have to send a ship, but—" Fox finished the thought with a significant grimace.

"Then, if I were you," Beach urged, "I wouldn't let Hayes get any wind of that side of the business."

"Hayes! Not a chance. Hayes will do what he's told, with Marion to handle him. And he'll find out just what we want him to find out. Marion will see to that. From the moment he left the island until we're done with him, Hayes won't stand any chance at all of learning things we don't want him to know. He's going to be handled as close as any dark horse that was ever sprung in the old racing days."

Beach nodded and shrugged. "It's none of my affair, of course. Business doesn't interest me, but I wonder—"

"What do you wonder?" Fox prompted when the sportsman stopped and looked dreamily across the room.

"I was just wondering—as a matter of purely academic interest—how this cave man Hayes, with all his queer ideas and ideals, is going to feel—when he finally discovers the way you have used him. I'm afraid—that will be—quite a shock to Hayes!"

Fox chuckled. "Maybe. What of it? Who gives a damn what Hayes thinks—or feels? Where does Hayes come in on this? He's just our sucker bait!"

Beach said earnestly: "Then, if I were you, Fox, I'd be very careful that Hayes doesn't find this out."

"Don't you worry! I am. Marion will see he doesn't find out. That's her job. You'll see the girl can handle Hayes as easy as she can use a powder puff!"

"I wonder!" Beach mused softly.

CHAPTER X

THE KINGDOM OF HOKUM

THE KINGDOM OF hokum exists wherever a trusting public pays its money at a ticket booth and enters a theater, town hall, or canvas tent to see persons and things that are not what they seem. Its national flag is as big as a circus sideshow banner, and its device is a group of snake charmers, Little Egypts, sea serpents and bearded ladies, above the motto: "Astounding—Mastodonic—Naughty."

The kingdom of hokum includes everything that isn't so—in art and in business—and its large population lives off the credulity of people so tired of commonplace living they will believe in anything. The theater is its greatest stronghold, but it must not be confused with the legitimate art of the theater, nor the legitimate in any art or business.

It is a parasite growth, sometimes charmingly colored, often amusing, and always useless. By general vote its capital is placed close to Broadway and Forty-Second Street on Manhattan Island. Three inventions—the camera, the electric light, and the printing press—have had much to do with making this strange growth great; and most important of the three is the printing press.

This intangible but very existent commonwealth a few years ago rejoiced in a beautiful woman who bathed every day in gallons of cream to preserve her beauty. It has been thrilled by a blue-shirted, diamond-in-the-rough "millionaire" miner of special-train, dollar-flinging fame, whose mine was all moonshine; and a Klondike queen that proved to be a lunch-room waitress from the Middle West. The names of its bogus nobility would fill a peerage many times as large as Burke's. Shooting showgirls are common as shooting stars in the Milky Way. It has, always, a plenty of explorers who never explored, actors who cannot act, poets who cannot rhyme, and authors whose best imaginative works are their own autobiographies. It is the place where scandals are a stock in trade, and men and women are precociously, absurdly skeptical of everything. The press agent, who goes by many euphonious titles, is its king.

On a drizzly evening when the particolored brilliance of the electric signs that are the aurora borealis of Broadway was repeated faithfully in the mirror of wet asphalt, a tall, commanding figure of a man clad in fur-hooded parka and arctic mukluks, followed by three hired porters who staggered under burdens of boxes and bales, shoved resolutely through the staring dinner crowds and entered a big hotel. Behind him followed a little queue of the bolder, more curious passers-by avid to see what new and strange was going to break out next.

At the reservation window the stranger gave his name, Jonathan Hayes, Kalvik Island, Alaska. As if the name was a signal, alert bellboys began to fight for the honor of carrying some small part of his baggage, for a reservation had been made for Jonathan Hayes: the most expensive and ornate suite in the house. There were already rumors about that his name stood for easy money.

It was dinner hour, and the lounge was filled with men and women awaiting appointments, idling, staring. When the procession that centered about Jonathan Hayes crossed the marble and gilt hall of huge columns and palms and shaded lights toward an elevator, hundreds of eyes followed it and a buzz of comment passed.

Under that machine-gun fire of glances and comments and smiles the big man, fantastically clad, bore himself with a poise like a king. His deeply tanned, sober face showed no sense of confusion nor embarrassment. His dark eyes observed and openly admired many marvels, but never admitted that the soul of the beholder was awed or belittled by a new world.

Jonathan Hayes of Kalvik, whose position was as strange and embarrassing as any earth man's, set down in the superior civilization of some distant planet, radiated an aurora of native dignity that commanded the scene and turned it immensely to his advantage.

Before he had got to the elevator an assistant manager of the hotel—no less—had taken charge of his caravan and commanded his progress.

An astute press agent of the same hotel, whose duty it was to see to things like this, already was busy at the telephone, dropping hints to city editors of morning newspapers that there was a "story" there in the shape of some sort of Eskimo prince— or something.

According to their habit, some derisively, some gently humorous, some prosy, the morning newspapers informed all the world that cared to read of the arrival of the man from Kalvik who never before had been in civilization. The story of his gold nugget tips, his princely gifts of furs and ivory and his fortune in sealskins was told. Best reading of all were the man's naive comments on the wonders of Broadway.

It was a cumulative news sensation, each day's development more interesting than the last, for the adroit mind of Marion Reade directed it, but from behind the scenes. It was Marion who wired to Jonathan Hayes, kept waiting outside the city, the exact hour for his entry, choosing a dull Sunday evening when the morning papers' columns were gaping for something new. It was Marion, still in the background for the time, who directed each day's activities, and Al Sapley, apparently a casual acquaintance of Hayes, who was her able lieutenant on the spot to see that events happened as she ordered.

In this way Jonathan Hayes became news—news worthy of the special writers and movie camera men from the topical weeklies. The dramatic story of his sealskins and his fight against

Cook on Kalvik Island was supplemented by the dramatic things he did and said in his new environment, until theaters were bidding for his favor at box parties, new charities seeking his attendance at drives for funds, new plays and stars demanding his criticism.

Jonathan Hayes's views on every topic of civilization—of which he knew nothing—were sought and considered as the views of an expert; his words were worth more than his gold nuggets; even his nod was valued as the recognition of a king, for publicity, skillfully managed, in a few days made a king of him—a king of the news.

Luck and skill combined kept him on front pages for three weeks. After that his news prominence was assured, and the weekly magazines, the motion pictures, and rotogravure newspapers kept him going—and set the stage for the manipulations of Douglas Fox.

Jonathan Hayes and Marion, Douglas Fox and his wife, Irving Beach and Al Sapley stepped out of Fox's limousine and pushed through Broadway crowds into a famous supper and dancing place.

Many heads were turned with their passing, for the face and figure of Jonathan Hayes were widely known now. He no longer wore fur-hooded parka and mukluks. Marion had ordered the change after ten days of publicity. "Don't keep him looking like a savage," she explained. "The wise ones are bound to guess he's got something to sell if he dresses all the time like an Indian medicine doctor. Give him dignity with individuality." So Hayes was not in conventional evening dress, but rough tweeds, with soft shirt and a wide-brimmed Stetson.

"Who's that—Bill Hart?" asked a man from Seattle, in the crowd.

His New York friend, showing him the town, answered proudly: "The man who bought Broadway."

"You don't mean Hayes, of Kalvik!"

"That's Hayes himself. Hurry. Let's crowd in and try to grab a table somewhere. Worthwhile sticking around where he is. He's liable to like a show girl and shower her with gold nuggets—or something. Always pulling something good. Let's go!"

Fox and his party seated themselves at the table reserved for them. The place was crowded, warm, noisy with the rhythm of jazz and talk and laughter. Toy balloons floated from many tables or drifted toward the ceiling, astray. Colored lights shone. There were women's bare shoulders in plenty and silk and gilt and jewels. The air mingled many scents.

"Toddle?" Beach asked of Marion invitingly.

Marion rose, smiling, and yielded herself to Beach's arms. They disappeared on the crowded dancing floor.

It was Beach's first appearance since they had parted in Seattle. Hayes, who had been trying all evening to get a few words with the sportsman, was disappointed again.

"Douglas," said Ada Fox, "maybe I'm getting old and fat, but you can dance with me still. Come on!"

Fox laughed. "I'll try anything once—even dancing with my wife."

"Well, sucker, how'd you like the show?" Sapley asked of Hayes. They had spent the evening at a *revue*.

Hayes, whose eyes had been watching Marion and Beach with thoughtful intentness, considered slowly. "It was beautiful—and nasty," he said. "Exquisite beauty and offensive vulgarity—as if somebody had defiled a fine statue with filth. And that last comedian, who told the stories those people roared at—that's the kind of man I could kill with my bare hands and enjoy it. Keep him out of my way!"

Sapley laughed shrilly.

"That's good! I happen to know the bird you speak of. He's one honest, hardworking poor fish with a wife and family. He owns a house out White Plains way and spends his days off playing with his kids. Sucker, don't you go making up your mind about anything you don't find out for yourself. F'rinstance! I saw you getting thick with Alma Lodestone, the singer, at that charity drive this afternoon. Figure she's a fine, home-loving, pie-baking dame, I suppose?"

"She's a fine, sincere woman," Hayes said firmly.

"You think so! I happen to know she got her training at the expense of a cloak and suit manufacturer on lower Broadway— and she paid for it the way most of these show girls do. And every step she's climbed since she's broke up a home and cost some John a pretty pile of jack!"

"You mean—"

"I mean exactly what you think I mean."

Hayes flushed angrily. "Sapley, I ought to knock you down for saying that!"

Sapley protested volubly. "I am not saying a word that isn't common knowledge and talk on Broadway. The divorce court records bear me out. God knows I'm the last man in the world to dish the dirt!"

The man from Kalvik brooded. He watched the dancers with a frown. "What ails all you people?" he burst out. "We savages up in Alaska believe in a man—or woman; take what they say as the truth—until we find out conclusively they have lied. Here, you seem to believe everybody a liar until he can prove he isn't—and I don't suppose you would believe him then! Your men have no integrity and your women no honor, if I can judge by what they say of each other—"

"No, you got us wrong there!" Al argued good naturedly. "We're like everybody else, part good and part bad in just about the same proportions. I guess the reason we're always so wise is that we're always getting stung! The worst sucker is always the guy that talks wisest—and that's the Broadway idea."

"Give me the Aleuts," Hayes growled. "I'm sick to death of believing everybody a liar!"

The dancers returned and ordered food and drink.

Beach sat himself next to Hayes. "What do you think of it all, now you've had a look?" he wanted to know.

Hayes shook his head.

"He's sore on all of us," Al interpreted. "Says we're all liars—and all the girls have got a past like a leopard skin—all spotted up."

"Don't take it too seriously," Beach advised, smiling gravely. "Some of us men are liars, most of us maybe, and the girls—well, some have spotted pasts and others invent spotted pasts because it makes good publicity. The real trouble is, Hayes, this isn't a world of grown-ups. We're children, terribly precocious children pretending and showing off. Remember that!"

"What he needs," Marion laughed into Hayes's sober face, "is to learn to jazz. Hayes, I'm going to teach you dancing next. Anybody gets sour that sits on the sidelines all the time!"

Hayes looked rebellious and she laughed louder. "Don't get scared. I won't teach you here—or tonight. But it's a shame to waste this music—"

"Toddle?" Beach invited, and she rose again and left them.

Hayes continued to glower. He was aware that a look passed between Sapley and Fox and Ada at Marion's second disappearance with Beach. Their heads went together and they whispered. Hayes caught a broken phrase or two: "—so would any girl. I'd jump at the chance myself," that was Ada speaking. "Hasn't Beach got everything a smart girl like her needs to put herself across?"

"She'll never lead that hard-boiled bird to the altar, and don't kid yourself," Sapley contributed. "Of course, if she isn't gunning for a marriage license—"

Fox said heavily, "The girl's private affairs are her own business, but she'd better not let 'em interfere with my business."

Hayes knew they were discussing Marion and Beach. Their frank impertinence made him furious. He wanted to denounce them for the slur their thoughts cast on Marion, but he hesitated. In his own mind there was a doubt, a very terrible doubt. The girl frankly avowed she used men to further her ambitions. It was ignoble of her. He should despise her for it. But he couldn't despise her because he loved her too dearly. Jealousy and this new-born suspicion of them all made him ill.

He recognized that Fox was speaking to him. "Got all the details fixed and the incorporation papers filed," Fox said. "We can spring the news on the public now whenever Marion thinks best. We'll get those sealskins of yours by next spring—"

"Not until spring!"

"Can't do everything at once. If we get enough stock sold and all by that time we'll break some recent speed records. Are you so keen to get back to Alaska?"

"Yes," said Hayes. "Right now I'd almost be willing to give up the whole thing to get back to Kalvik."

"Back to Kalvik!" Marion had come back in time to hear the last remark. "Hayes! So soon? You want to go back—"

"I do."

"Back to greasy Indians—and raw fish—and men like Cook."

"Yes, even Cook—" Hayes began with bitterness. "What is it?" he exclaimed, roused by the change in Marion's face.

The girl was looking across the big room and her eyes were round and frightened. She grew white. Her hand groped unsteadily for the back of a chair, as if she needed support.

Fox, Ada, all of them sprang up, crowding about her with exclamations. Marion said nothing, but stared fascinated.

Hayes followed the direction of her gaze with his own and without any word of explanation left the table and started across the cafe in the direction of the door.

Hayes took a straight line course and he went with a long, swift stride, blind to everything about him. He brushed a table and sent crockery and glass crashing. A chair tipped over and his shoulders caught a man who had risen hurriedly to protest, sending him spinning. He passed from the tables across the crowded dancing-floor and in his wake he left a commotion. Angry cries, a half-suppressed scream by a woman, a scuffling of feet that was not dancing rose above the thudding and braying of the orchestra. All over the place people were jumping to their feet to see what was happening. Waiters came running with undignified haste.

"Good God, he's gone mad!" Fox puffed. "They're both cuckoo!"

At the entrance to the place a small crowd of guests was backed up, some waiting for escort to their tables, others for a chance to get tables. Hayes plunged into this crowd with a shout that could be heard in the street outside.

There was a commotion at the rear of the crowd. A short, chunky man stepped quickly out of the throng and went through the outer door into the Broadway night.

Hayes followed him at a run.

Al Sapley had darted across the room after the big Alaskan. The cafe was riotous with men and women trying to follow Hayes's tumultuous progress, and others trying to crowd out of his way. The orchestra stopped in mid-bar. The confusion was now an uproar.

Beach pressed Marion into a chair. "What's up?" he asked.

"Dearie! For God's sake, tell us what happened!" Ada implored her.

Marion whispered shakily, "Cook!"

"Cook?" Fox looked bewildered. "Oh! That fellow that came to the island? What about Cook—"

"Cook is in this place. I saw him at the door. Hayes will kill him!"

"Damn!" Fox exclaimed, and threw himself into the scrimmage about the door.

"Are you sure?" Beach argued. "How could it be him?"

"Why, dearie, you're dreaming," Ada insisted. "That happened thousands of miles from here—"

"Do you think I could ever forget that man?" Marion exclaimed. "That was Captain Darius Cook. Hayes knew him—"

"Good Lord, somebody ought to tell the police. He's wanted for two killings," Beach exclaimed. "Here, waiter! Where's a telephone?"

CHAPTER XI

A FAMILIAR FACE

JONATHAN HAYES PLOWED through the astonished group about the door and burst out of the supper place with a rush. He hurled himself into the throng that packed the Broadway pavement, a crowd that moved slowly because of its own bulk. Good natured, talkative, laughing idlers poured forth from the theaters. Into this throng he had seen the unmistakable bald head of Darius Cook disappear.

Hayes made a bee-line in the same direction, and his weight and speed forced a way as if he had been a cannon-ball. Yet when he got to the curb, in which direction Cook undoubtedly was headed, there was no sign of the man.

His startling advent, hatless, grim, fighting mad and oblivious of everything, resulted in a contagion of excitement that did not stop at the cafe door. He was speedily ringed by a curious crowd that definitely ended all hope of catching a glimpse of the fugitive Cook.

Noise of the excitement drifted from the doorway he had just quit, and a bareheaded waiter ran out, followed by men and women in evening dress.

Hayes, who had accepted defeat without waste of emotion, turned back to the supper place and found himself in the grip of a patrolman, several clamoring witnesses ready to accuse him of anything from assault and battery to manslaughter.

Fortunately at that moment Al Sapley caught up with events. It was Al who calmed the troubled waters and persuaded patrolman, guests, and waiters to return inside, where the matter could be settled peaceably, by apologies, tips and the offer to make good any damage. The recognition accorded Jonathan Hayes made a simple matter of it. A cave man must be expected to do something wild occasionally.

Hayes, far from being the censured culprit, found himself acclaimed as soon as he was generally recognized. He declined a half-dozen invitations to drink from pocket flasks and to join various parties at other tables. Even those whose toes he had trod upon seemed to consider it an honor.

"That's what proper publicity does!" Fox exclaimed to Sapley. "That fellow's a popular hero!"

"But what is Cook doing here?" Beach worried. "The man is dangerous!"

"For a dangerous guy he's a fast runner!" Sapley chuckled.

Fox snorted. "Was it Cook?" he sneered. "If so, what of it?"

"If so, he's probably on the trail of your sealskins," said Beach. "Remember, he's a bad lot!"

"You will stick to your movie plot, Beach! If it's Cook after those skins I'll say he goes to a lot more trouble than I would. But, one thing—there ought to be good publicity in this. I'll talk to Marion." Marion greeted the idea with a shudder. "You can laugh," she exclaimed, "but Cook isn't any joke to me. And that was Cook. And he doesn't mean any good to any of us—"

"Save that for the newspapers," Fox laughed. "Don't try to kid me!"

"I'm not. And I can see about as much humor in making publicity out of Cook as I can in petting a rattlesnake. Still, as you say, it is a good story!"

The evening papers of the next day carried the story. Long before their press hour Marion had recovered her instinct to make publicity, even out of Cook. But she argued with Sapley and Fox that all of them must be on their guard against surprises.

Every day there came a large number of letters addressed to

Jonathan Hayes of Kalvik. They were letters of all sorts, advertising circulars, beguiling propositions from stock brokers who had sure-thing tips, offers to let him into all sorts of new schemes, offers of theatrical and lecture contracts and a number of plain begging letters.

A part of Al Sapley's duties was to read them all and advise Hayes about them. Many went into the waste-basket and Hayes was none the wiser.

In the same way Al Sapley, in the guise of secretary and best friend, saw Hayes's callers before Hayes did, and winnowed out the desirable from the undesirable.

"We can't afford to waste money," Fox directed. "If our wild man gives away a seal pelt or an ivory tusk or a nugget it's our business to see he gives it where it will bring in returns. I'm no Santa Claus, buying all this junk to waste it!"

The consequence was that between Marion and Sapley, Hayes was a prisoner, but not quite conscious of it. His life was supervised every hour of it, but it was done skillfully in order not to offend him or rouse active rebellion. He was a free man still, in his own opinion.

Late in the afternoon, several days after the excitement in the cafe, Hayes came back to his hotel suite, thoroughly tired with participation in a benefit performance for a widely advertised charity. He told Al Sapley he meant to sleep before dinner. Sapley was glad to get away on his own business. For once there was nobody about to censor the activities of the tamed cave man.

Hayes was stretched on a couch, half asleep when the telephone rang insistently. Instinctively he looked about for Sapley or Marion to answer it, remembered they were not there and took the receiver off its hook with a little thrill at the novelty of it. The talking wires Hayes still regarded with something that was almost superstitious reverence.

"This is the key clerk on your floor," the voice said. "A young woman brought a note for you and left it with me. Shall I send it in?"

"Mr. Sapley looks after those things."

The key clerk, a woman, hesitated momentarily. "The young woman said this was very important. She wanted you to read it personally. Was quite anxious about it. Of course, if you wish it to wait—"

"Send it to me," Hayes directed.

Presently a boy handed him the note. It was sealed in a pink envelope that looked soiled from much handling. The address was in rounding characters, a little straggling, suggesting a juvenile hand. Hayes read:

> I wonder if you remember last Monday how you talked to a girl that wore an old green cape when you were going around with that bunch of charity visitors from the Neighborhood Association? You said, Mr. Hayes, if there was ever anything you could do for me I was to let you know, and I have been trying to let you know four times now, but you don't ever seem to get my letters. It's not for me, Mr. Hayes, that I'm asking anything, but there is an Indian boy is staying in the tenement I live in, and he's pretty sick. He says he is from your country and has heard about the good you do for Indians, and if you was to hear about him you could help him out. So I am writing this to ask you to come and see this boy, and if you can come before six o'clock tonight I will be waiting for you at the Twenty-Third Street station of the Ninth Avenue L to show you where the boy is. I told the Indian boy you would surely come, and he is expecting you.
>
> Your friend,
> NATALIE SMITH.

Hayes made his decision without waste of time. Come? Of course he would come! The Aleuts never had sent for him in vain in their own land. Now that one of them lay ill in this strange city of greed and ignorance and calloused indifference to the suffering stranger, certainly he would not deny his wish!

He was very glad of the chance to do something for somebody—something which Marion or Fox or Al had no hand in. He was glad to do something for anybody, for action would put aside for the time thoughts he had in mind—not very pleasant thoughts.

The prospect of speaking to one of his own Indians in the familiar tongue reminded him how much alone he really was in this new world.

He rode on the Elevated railway to Twenty-Third Street and came down the station steps very much interested and excited. A young woman who wore a faded green cape met him at the foot of the iron stair and led him down Twenty-Third Street toward the river.

"I just knew you'd come, if you got my letter," she exclaimed.

"Who is this boy? What is his name?"

"I can't make head or tail of it. It sounds like Oo-ten-na to me—"

"That's probably just what it is. Where is he from? How did he get here. Who—"

"Say, listen! You've got to ask him all that. I don't know. He's had a little hall room in the house I live in and he got sick and I was going to tell the cop that he'd ought to be taken away in the ambulance—but he felt so bad I said I'd try to speak to you about it. That's all I know. Honest!"

"That was a fine thing to do," Hayes exclaimed. He glanced at the girl with more interest. He could see little of her, but a sallow face half covered by an absurdly large hat and the voluminous green cape, from which unbelievably thin legs extended. She looked like thousands of girls he had seen these last few weeks: thin, pert, all of a size and type.

When they came to Tenth Avenue, where freight cars were being hauled past in the dusk and big trucks thundered over the cobbles, the girl took Hayes's arm and guided him. It was too noisy to talk. They turned south for several blocks and then west again into a frowzy cross-street of warehouses, garages and a few old red brick tenements.

Before the dark door of one of these the girl stopped and used a latch-key. To Hayes, unused to such places, there was nothing strange in the action nor anything strange in the darkness of the house.

A gas jet burned very dimly in the hall she led him into and the street door slammed behind them.

"It's up those stairs, second floor, the end room in the back of the hall just as you go up," the girl said. She seemed a little out of breath.

Hayes paused as he mounted the stairs. "Aren't you coming?" he asked.

She was watching him from below.

"Unh-uh! You better talk to him alone. Go up. You'll see a light in the room—"

"I'd like to talk to you again—" Hayes began, but the girl had disappeared somewhere in the dark hall. As he went up he heard the slam of a distant door and noted the peculiar, hollow reverberation it made—a noise suggestive of an empty house.

In the hall above there was another gas jet burning, turned very low, like the first, and near the head of the stair one of several doors stood slightly ajar. A dim light came through the crack.

Hayes knocked at the door and said, in Aleut, "Oo-ten-na, this is a friend come to see you."

A muffled voice answered in the same tongue, "I am glad. Come in."

Hayes entered the room and saw a cot-bed against the wall, on which lay a man covered with a blanket. But even as he entered the light in the room vanished.

"That light is blown out again!" the man on the bed exclaimed in Aleut. "Close the door and make a light."

Hayes turned to close the door.

The shadows of the room stirred with life.

Half a dozen men leaped for Hayes at the same time as if his turning had been their signal.

He was borne to the floor and the assailants went down with him, making a terrific thudding on the bare boards.

As a surprise the attack was completely successful. But Jonathan Hayes, in spite of the surprise, was giving his attackers plenty to think about.

The tangled heap of human forms heaved and rolled over, and somebody broke the silence with a hoarse bellow: "My arm! Oh, God!"

A man was thrown across the room and met the wall with a crash.

The form covered with a blanket rose suddenly from the bed and lighted the gas jet. The flame flooded the room with light and revealed the man who had struck the match and stood aside from the fight now, watching. It was Captain Darius Cook, dapper and cool as of old.

Yet the dapper captain sprang suddenly onto the writhing men and caught an arm that had raised a clubbed pistol with the evident intention of braining Hayes. His strong fingers twisted the helpless wrist, and the pistol dropped.

Cook deliberately aimed several swift, well-placed kicks at the man who had raised the weapon. He reached down and caught him, twisting his shirt-collar into a noose that strangled him. Thus Cook disengaged the fighter and brought him to his feet, backing him against the wall, where he bumped his head repeatedly to emphasize his mild reproof.

"I said you were not to hurt this man. This is not a murder. Perhaps you will remember that. Yes?"

Cook flung his henchman aside and the man crumpled up, half dead of strangulation, over the quiet form already flung against the side of the room. The captain dusted his hands daintily and turned back to watch the fight.

The writhing group had quieted. Hayes was spread-eagled, flat against the floor. One man each clung to his legs and arms. All of them were breathing hard, and that was all the sound there was for a moment.

"Please bring his wrists together," Cook directed amiably. They managed that by hard work. The captain bent low and snapped steel handcuffs over Hayes's wrists.

"Now the legs," he said. Steel hobbles linked by a chain were made fast to the prisoner's legs.

"Let him up," Cook ordered.

They let go, and Hayes bounded to his feet as if a spring had been released. He sprang at Cook, his manacled hands raised above his head. If the blow had fallen Cook would have been brained.

But the captain dodged and caught the blow of the murderous manacles on his shoulder. Before Hayes could strike again the other four had seized him.

Cook had been staggered by the blow, but he maintained his unnatural serenity, though his greenish eyes had an unholy incandescence of their own.

"Good gracious!" he gasped. "Somebody tie this man into that chair. Really, you mustn't be so rough, Hayes!"

The four of them forced Hayes into a wooden chair, and one of them produced rope with which they lashed him fast. He was helpless now, doubled into the chair and tied there. He sat still at last, glaring at Cook.

"Well," said Cook cheerfully, "that's better. Turn him around so I can sit here on the bed and have a little talk with him. And you—all of you—can get out. Take those two with you." He pointed out the two injured men. "Stay in the hall—but not too near that door."

Cook saw personally that his orders were carried out. Then he returned and seated himself on the cot, facing Hayes.

"Now we can talk quietly," he announced, "but not in Aleut!" He grinned at the joke.

"I have nothing to say to you," Hayes panted.

"Oh, yes, you have! Oh, dear me, yes! And, really, this is a much safer place to talk than Kalvik. There, there was always danger of interruptions—yachts, revenue cutters—all sorts of things. Here, with millions of people crowded around us, there are never interruptions. People mind their own business in New York."

"What do you want of me?"

"Guess!" Cook was playfully ironic.

CHAPTER XII

ONE HONEST MAN
WARNS ANOTHER

JONATHAN HAYES, MANACLED, hobbled and bound to the chair Cook's men had forced him into, managed to meet Cook's complacence with a very fair complacence of his own. "If you hurry, I dare say you can murder me without any interruption, Cook."

"No hurry!" Cook smiled. "No hurry at all. And, my dear chap, I do wish you wouldn't be crude—"

"You'll never find out from me where those sealskins are hid."

"No, Hayes? Really! 'Never' is a long time. Consider. This is a nice, quiet spot, surrounded by something like four or five million people—I think the larger figure is nearer correct. I have taken pains that we sha'n't be disturbed here. And, as I said, the chance of interruption from outsiders is *nil*. Really, Hayes, you must understand that the average New Yorker does not go about interfering in other people's business. Civilization has taught him that he has troubles enough managing his own affairs.

"If I choose to, I can murder you by slow torture, or cut you into fine pieces, or boil you in oil, or pick your eyes out, and lop off your fingers, one by one. Not that I would like to do any of those things to you, Hayes. Good gracious, no!"

Cook paused and grinned his thin-lipped, sardonic grin. In the gaslight, his bald head sparsely covered with the wet plastered strands of red hair, the man looked like a vulture—indecent and unclean. Hayes loathed him.

"I'm not going to tell you anything," he repeated angrily.

"I don't ask it," said Cook.

The helpless man stared and opened his mouth and eyes in comical surprise.

"No. Honestly, Hayes, I brought you her to tell you something. Sounds queer, I suppose, taking all this trouble, but that's my intention. I want you to listen to me. Forget for the minute that you have cause to feel annoyed and cross with me. I am serious. I wonder, Hayes, if you've discovered yet that I am an honest man?"

"You honest!"

Cook was undisturbed by his scorn.

"Yes, I am," he repeated. "As honest as you are—and I want to explain that. Old chap, think a minute. Did you ever have any doubt as to my motives?"

"None," Hayes answered promptly and bitterly. "I always knew you for a murderer and blackleg—"

"Well," Cook said with a shrug, "that's not quite the point. But you always knew I meant to get those sealskins. I never made a secret of that, did I? Didn't I offer you a partnership—"

"In my own sealskins!"

"But you needed me—and need me now, worse than ever you did. I was frank about what I wanted. You were frank in your refusal. *Hayes, that's more than Fox and his crowd are.*"

"What are you getting at?"

"Just this—you're in the hands of crooks and thieves and liars. You, an honest man! Yes, I'm serious about this. As another honest man, I warn you—"

"Warn me!" Hayes wondered if the man was insane.

"Yes, warn you! Warn you against Douglas Fox and his choice gang of swindlers. You poor innocent, haven't you, even yet, the slightest idea of what they are doing to you—of what their game is? Have you no idea of the way Fox is exploiting you—"

"Cook, are you crazy, or am I? I—this doesn't make any sense. Fox is organizing a company to get the sealskins. What of it?"

"To get the sealskins!" Cook repeated, and laughed with fine sarcasm. "Oh, come—you still believe that?"

"Certainly I believe that! I know—"

"Organizing a company to sell stock, you mean. To sell stock to silly, ignorant, gullible fools. To rob widows and orphans of their savings—to cheat and defraud. You—and the sealskins; do you know what part you play in this? You're the bait—that's all. You're the figurehead, the brass band, the big bass drum that advertises his swindle—that's what you are. And you still maintain this childish belief that Fox is going to send a ship to get your sealskins. Oh, this is good!"

Cook laughed silently and with very good relish.

"You are innocent!" he burst out.

Hayes's face began to redden. He could outface Cook in the matter of defiance, but the attack had taken an unexpected angle that surprised him completely.

"I suppose," Cook sneered, "you thought you came to New York of your own free will? I suppose you still think you are your own master? That you walk down Broadway dressed like a circus horse because you like to play the fool? That you give away a basketful of silly tourist souvenirs every day because you like to play Santa Claus? You do all these things in the belief they have some connection with getting those skins? You're serious about it? Good God!"

Hayes's surprise left him confused. There was something in the way Cook said these things, a conviction of their truth, that made him believe them. Never had he been as completely at the mercy of Cook as this moment. The man's new weapon broke down all his defenses for the time.

Suspicion of Douglas Fox and his associates never had occurred to him before. He had done as they had asked, and done it willingly. Often the things that they made him do seemed idiotic to Hayes, but he was in a new world, in the hands of friends, in Marion's hands. He trusted everything to Marion.

A gull? An ignorant, innocent fool—Shown off like a dancing bear on a chain for the amusement of Broadway and to serve some crooked scheme of Douglas Fox's?

He had never thought of that!

Cook had him completely at his mercy. It was in his power to do a great deal with Jonathan Hayes. But Cook made a mistake. He leaned forward and laid his hand on Hayes's knee, a persuasive gesture meant to enforce what he was about to say.

At the touch of Cook's hand something chilled Hayes. The confusion of his thoughts was clarified almost instantly. A great draft of fresh air seemed to blow through his brain, and it blew away the smoke and gases of this newborn doubt of Fox and himself.

"My dear chap," Cook smiled gently, "they have been playing you for a fool! The only question is, will you stand for it, or are you man enough to revolt? You may dislike me—not without some cause—you may distrust me; but admit, at least, I dealt honestly. I never tried to make a fool of you. And I'm willing to offer you the same terms I offered before—a fifty-fifty partnership—if you will show me where those pelts are hid."

It was Hayes's turn to laugh now. "You were a long time coming to that. But you came out just where I looked to find you, Cook."

Cook looked at him sharply, surprised by his change of manner. "What! You don't believe what I have told you?"

"My good, honest man," said Hayes with significant and scornful emphasis, "I do not."

"You will let Fox make a laughing-stock of you? Dress you up like a circus clown, put you through your tricks, and then kick you aside like an old shoe, when he has swindled all the gulls you attract!"

Hayes smiled and shook his head gently. "Cook, you are so transparent with all this stuff! So simple. Fool that I am, even

I can see your motive—your wonderful philanthropic desire to take me into partnership and rob me at your leisure. If I were you—"

Cook flushed now. For once he lost his easy manner. He saw he had lost, and it made him rage.

"Fool!" he screamed. "Idiot! Blockhead! Oh—you fool! You prefer to let them exploit you—and lose everything!"

"If I were you," Hayes began again, "I'd go back to simple, honest methods that you seem so fond of. Try torturing me if you think that it will get you anything."

"You let them play you for a fool!" Cook shouted. "You'll wear their collar and run around on a chain wherever that flip, painted, yellow-haired—"

"Stop!" Hayes shouted. "I warn you that—"

But Cook was fairly frothing. "A man—a man like you, letting himself be led about! The newest freak pet of a common Broadway show girl, a—"

Hayes was manacled and hobbled and made fast to the chair, but his feet had restricted liberty. He hurled himself, chair and all, upon Cook and bore the captain down on the cot.

The blow deprived Cook of wind for a moment; then he began to struggle, and his fists lashed out. Hayes, perfectly helpless, had to take the blows. He managed to roll over and hide his face.

Cook sprang to his feet then and began to rain blows with better direction. His fingers found Hayes's throat and were choking him.

The men from the hall ran in. They closed in about the struggling figures. Hayes was able to lash out short kicks with his hobbled feet. He had no other means of defense, and they speedily had him helpless and upright again.

While a man held him at either side Cook stepped up and struck him deliberately in the face. His lips had writhed back, baring his teeth. The man grimaced horribly. For the moment he seemed insane in his fury.

At the blow Hayes lunged again, and his guards were dragged to one side and the other. Cook danced back lightly out of reach, grinning without mirth. The others sprang to help hold the prisoner.

Another sound, loud and insistent, made itself heard and felt above their turmoil. Somewhere in the house a window crashed in, then a second.

In the room they became quickly silent—so silent that they could hear the tinkle of belated fragments of glass, then the sound of heavy footsteps.

A voice from below shouted frantically, screechingly, "Hayes! Hayes!"

Al Sapley's voice!

"Here!" Hayes roared. "Second floor!" Then he lunged again at his captors.

But his captors had something else to think about—their own safety. Cook addressed them briefly. "Get out," he said. The six vanished from the room, finding some exit prepared in advance.

Cook lingered but a moment more to glare at Hayes.

"Some day, Hayes, when you know the truth, you'll realize what an utter damn fool you've been today."

Having said that, Cook stepped to the window, threw up its sash, and crawled out. His hands lingered a moment, clinging to the sill, then let go. He had dropped to the roof of a low extension at the rear.

Al Sapley and three armed men burst into the room almost simultaneously.

Hayes roared at Al: "Cook! Out that window!"

"After him, two of you!" Sapley directed.

Hayes saw them hesitate.

"Baldheaded man," he added for their instruction. "Red beard. Short. Now hustle."

They nodded, understanding, and crawled out of the window

in pursuit. Sapley sent his third man after the others, and he himself began to untangle Hayes from the chair, babbling exclamations and questions as he worked. Hayes told him the story briefly as, together, they took part in the hunt for Cook.

Cook had disappeared effectively. In the dark and drizzle, and sheltered by a maze of backyard fences, wagon sheds, junk yards and rookeries, escape was comparatively simple for him, Hayes and Sapley returned empty handed and discouraged to the house. There they found one man of Cook's gang had been arrested, the worst hurt of the lot.

"Just about what I expected!" Sapley declared disgustedly after the prisoner had been cross-questioned. "A cheap gangster, hired for the job. He doesn't know what it's all about and doesn't care. He's working for his fifteen dollars a day and it don't matter to him whether the job is abduction or murder—so long as he gets paid."

"And the girl who brought that note to me?"

"Hired for the job, of course, hired by Cook."

"You don't think, then, they will ever find Cook?" Hayes asked.

"Yes, about the time they find Charley Ross—but I guess you never heard of Charley Ross; eh, sucker?"

Al grinned affectionately on the big Alaskan.

"You probably saved me from an unpleasant death," Hayes said gratefully. "But I don't understand yet how you happened to find me at all?"

Sapley looked slightly confused for a moment. "Oh, a friend of mine saw you go out—and got kind of curious," he murmured. "He knew you didn't know the town, and it sort of worried him. He called me up on the phone and told me—and I hotfooted it after you. Brought these other birds along. They're special officers from a detective bureau."

So far as it went Al's explanation was true enough. He omitted to mention that his mysterious and observing "friend" was a private detective, one of several, hired to watch Hayes at all times and to report his movements whenever Hayes's usual associates were not with him. This quiet surveillance was one of Douglas Fox's precautions to keep the cave man from straying into embarrassing complications.

In effect, it made Hayes, all unconscious of it, as much a prisoner as if he were behind bars.

CHAPTER XIII

INTRIGUES

THE MORNING AFTER the attack on Hayes, Douglas Fox sent for Marion. The promoter maintained a handsome office suite on Forty-Second Street, and his inner sanctum had all the massive, rich solid look that should go with wealth and power. The furniture was copied from museum pieces—high-backed chairs elaborately carved, fit for a throne room, and an antique Italian table as big as Fox's limousine. There were rugs and one or two well-chosen pictures; there were pearl buttons for Fox to push when he wanted an office boy or stenographer. The business betrayed itself by one modest sign on the door— *Douglas Fox, Inc.*

The promoter had morning papers spread all over his big Italian table. When Marion came in he was poring over them.

"Today we spring our company on a waiting world," Fox announced cheerfully. "It's absolutely the right moment. This morning's story of Hayes and his mysterious enemies is the final touch. The suckers are ripe for it."

Marion seemed about to say something, but Fox went on: "I've got a kind of hunch for things like this. Experience, I suppose. Don't know much about publicity. Couldn't write even an ad that would give away movie tickets to the kids. I'm crude. But I can feel in my bones when it's time for suckers to bite. Learned it with a medicine show, and I never forget. This stock will sell—sell like Liberty Bonds in war time—"

"I want to talk to you about this," Marion interrupted. She

sat down, facing Fox. She looked at him long and searchingly. She asked finally: "You are bound to go through with this your own way?"

"What d'you mean—my own way?"

"You know what I mean. You're determined this is a stock selling chance and nothing more?"

Fox laughed loudly and good humoredly. "You too!" he exclaimed. "Marion, I thought you were too hard-boiled to fall for your own line of hokum!"

"I'm not falling for my own line of hokum! But I think I've still got common sense enough to detect signs of the truth when I run into them—"

"Meaning?"

"Meaning, why don't you go into this on the level?"

"That's about enough of that!" Fox said, turning red. "Nobody can say I'm not on the level. Nobody. And that goes for you."

"Tosh!" Marion's eyes flashed. "Tell that to suckers! If you mean you're not going to break any laws, say so. I know you won't—for the darn good reason it isn't healthy. But you're not on the level with the boobs who buy stock in your company, and you're not on the level with Hayes. None of us are. If you were you'd raise enough to send a ship after his seal pelts without going into any stock selling scheme."

"What would I get out of that!"

"A share in the profits—"

"If there are any! Supposing of course the skins are there, and in good condition and can be sold. Supposing all that, I might earn enough to buy gas for my car all of next year—if I was lucky!" Fox sneered. "What's got into you, anyhow?" he exclaimed.

"Nothing—except it just struck me that Hayes— Well, we're handing Hayes a pretty raw deal—"

"Hayes been talking to you?" Fox demanded eagerly. "Did you get this idea from Hayes?"

"Well, you know you wanted to find out just what happened between Cook and Hayes. Asked me to find out—"

"Yes, yes! Well, go on—"

She hesitated. "I did find out—"

"Atta girl! Well?"

She went on with evidence of a spiteful satisfaction in her news, that made her brown eyes snap. "Douglas, look out you don't get so hard boiled and wise that you make a sucker of yourself, sometime. This man Cook, whom you seem to regard solely as a dispensation of Providence to give your scheme publicity, isn't to be sneezed at!"

"Poof! A roughneck and some hired gangsters! He's been reading dime novels!"

"Yes?" said Marion sweetly. "Well anyhow, instead of trying anything crude on Hayes, this time he told him a little wholesome truth about you—and all of us. And it's got Hayes worrying!"

Fox's heavy-featured, handsome face lost some of its complacence. He looked a little frightened as he stared hard at the girl across the table, a smartly tailored girl, wearing a small, close fitting street hat of felt from beneath which her short cut hair of gold curled delightfully. Marion evidently enjoyed the effect of her words.

"Did Cook knock us to Hayes?"

"As nearly as I can get it, he told Hayes some bitter truth—"

"And Hayes? Is he sore? Does he believe it? Will you stop playing mystery and tell me what in hell Hayes said!"

"Hayes doesn't want to believe it," Marion answered slowly. Fox sighed heavily as if that took a load off his shoulders. "He'll stick, then? He'll go through?"

"He's loyal—because he thinks that you—and me—all of us—are his friends. Cook, in spite of the fact you think him a fat head, warned Hayes exactly of what you plan to do. And it worries him. But he told me, loyally. He said he wouldn't believe a word of it, because *we are his friends.* Douglas, that big hick is trusting you!"

Fox smote his knee noisily. "Good enough!" he exclaimed, grinning. "Well then, everything's all right. Good Lord—for a minute you had me jumping sideways! Why, it's all right, then!"

Marion studied him thoughtfully with disgusted calculation. She had thought perhaps news of Hayes's confiding trust might stir a little sympathy in Fox's heart. It hadn't stirred anything more noticeable than a feeling of relief that his scheme was not in danger. Yet Fox was not disloyal to his associates. He didn't double-cross them! Probably, she reasoned, he could never be made to regard Hayes as a human being—one of his own kind. Hayes was something to be exploited—a different race entirely.

But Hayes's childlike faith had touched Marion more than she would admit. She alone inspired that faith. She realized it with a little fright and uneasiness. In her hands the man was wax, to be molded as she chose.

Hayes had called her a "tinsel woman" and had treated her as something worthless. Her vow was to make him pay. She would show him just how dangerous a tinsel woman could be if you got her sore! And she was showing him, here on her own ground—Broadway. Hayes was jumping the hurdles as she cracked the whip. She was making good her boast to deliver him, postage paid. But she hadn't counted on the demoralizing effect the daily evidence of the big fellow's absolute trust in her might have. When Hayes told her of the interview with Cook a thought had come, unbidden. "What a rotten lot we are! The only place he gets the truth is from Cook—who's out to cut his throat! Isn't there anybody—anybody at all—to protect the poor fish?"

Fox leaned across the table and took her hands in his. "Good girl," he applauded, "Good kid! I'm not forgetting, Marion, that I owe it to you if this goes over big! I'm not forgetting for a minute that it's you who keep Hayes in line. He's your cave man—and he eats out of your hand. You're a damn smart girl, and believe you me, you won't lose by it. When it comes to the split you'll find there's a fat bonus for you!"

Marion's voice jangled as she cried vehemently, "For God's sake, Fox, don't talk about money! Don't remind me again what I'm getting out of this!"

"All right, all right," Fox protested soothingly. "Got a little katzenjammer this morning, eh? Take it easy today. You work too hard. All nerves!"

During her busy day a ghost stood at Marion's elbow, the phantom presentiment of Jonathan Hayes. She heard it repeat, "Of course Cook is a liar, I don't believe these things of you— or Fox—or any of you. I'm trusting the whole thing to you—and just your word is good enough for me." And the phantom kept repeating this; the look in his eyes as he said it would not vanish.

She must be all nerves today, as Fox had said. In the late afternoon she was glad of the chance to get away, out into the sharp air and the crowds, determined to lose the phantom by a brisk walk.

Characteristically she chose Fifth Avenue for the promenade, and starting from her studio in a quiet old building on Sixteenth Street she swung briskly up the crowded pavement. The level rays of late sun made pure gold of the spires and towers of buildings along the wide thoroughfare. In the depth between lay a deep shadow of rich, luminous blue through which moved the long vista of great crowds and traffic; limousine and taxi tops glistened with reflected light; big green buses in long lines, like herds of strange circus elephants lumbered along slowly, making frequent stops; traffic towers glowed white, and green, and red, as they ruled the vast, lively throng.

Slender, erect, brisk, her jolly little hat pressed tight over the short, curling gold hair, her neatly tailored bronze tweeds with fur about the throat, making of her a splendid, soldierly little figure, Marion shouldered along at a good gait. She threaded the business section of lower Fifth, the cloak and suit region of the Twenties and so into the shopping, spending, idling district of hotels and big stores and exclusive shops and art galleries. She passed the library and the town's chief cross artery, and still was walking briskly—but the shade of Hayes was ever at her shoulder.

"I'm trusting the whole thing to you," it kept saying. When she could put that out of mind Fox's praises repeated themselves, "You're a damn smart girl, and you won't lose by it."

She almost collided with a man strolling more leisurely; it was Beach, who skillfully drew her out of the throng, voicing his delight at the encounter.

Marion heard herself saying to Beach, "And I wanted to see you. Been wanting to talk to you. How about this pastry place? Shall we have tea?"

They found a little booth in the shop. Of the several men who turned their heads to watch that smart little figure pass and envy Beach, two were Hayes and Sapley, also strolling.

"There's our Marion—with Beach again!" Al exclaimed. "Sucker, there's something doing there!"

"I saw them," Hayes acknowledged briefly.

Al looked at him studiously for a moment, wondering. "Takes it hard! Wonder if the big hick's really jealous?"

"Anything you have to say to me is just like a Christmas present," Beach smiled, when Marion and he were served.

"I—" Marion hesitated. "I haven't quite made up my mind what I'm going to say—or whether to say it. If I do, it's not the sort of thing to discuss here."

Beach looked surprised in spite of his effort not to show his curiosity.

"Surely, you wouldn't hesitate in telling me—anything?"

"No—not if I were sure—sure I ought to, I mean. I—suppose I make sure. What are you doing this evening?"

"Whatever you say, Marion."

"Will you come to my studio about eleven o'clock? I have some work earlier in the evening. Can you do that?"

"Certainly," Beach agreed. "I'll be there." He was plainly curious now.

Marion smiled gratefully. "You *are* a good pal! And—if I disappoint you—if it turns out I haven't anything to say, after all, promise not to feel sore about it!" Beach promised. "This begins to sound like something deep," he smiled.

"It is," Marion said earnestly. "I feel that way about it, anyhow. But let's forget about it now—so I'll have a chance to think it out straight!"

She was regretting her impulse already. Her mind had been so filled with Hayes she had spoken without thought—and she didn't believe in doing that sort of thing—not for a minute! "It just shows how things are getting my goat!" she thought, censuring herself.

She dined at a hotel with Fox and his wife and Hayes. The Foxes danced and Hayes was left a few moments alone with her.

"I'll certainly have to teach you to toddle!" Marion declared.

Hayes answered seriously, "I suppose I'll have to learn."

"And you dread it?"

"No. Not that. I was thinking about something—about that night I came aboard the yacht and I told you I loved you—and asked for the chance to prove myself against your civilization. I didn't realize then what a big thing I was going against! It is a big thing, a terrifying thing—"

"You mean it's got you whipped?"

"No; it's got me wondering. I'm wondering if I'm quite as big as I thought I was. Marion, tell me, have I made any progress—or has this world of yours simply made a fool of me? Is there any hope for me at all?"

Marion answered him heartily: "Stuff! Nobody—nothing can make a fool of a man—unless he agrees to be made a fool of. Buck up!"

But his strange humility touched her deeply. There was doubt and mistrust in Hayes's look and attitude—mistrust of himself—and an appeal. She knew then that her stopping of Beach that afternoon had not been a mistake. She began to see what it was she wanted to talk to Beach about.

CHAPTER XIV

AL SAPLEY APOLOGIZES

MARION'S STUDIO WAS in a sober-looking building that dated back to a day when space in New York was cheap, when even a business office was a sizable room—as large, say, as two modern apartments. There were no elevators, but a stairway of shallow steps and massive oak balustrade as broad as some streets. The halls, too, were spacious, and the rooms had high ceilings and deep windows.

It was a pleasant, businesslike sort of room, with Marion's flat-topped desk in a comer near a window, and a steel letter-file case and hooded typewriter to speak for her industry. The rest was homelike, with a touch of her peculiar profession in places in the shape of photographs autographed by various famous persons grateful for the publicity she had won them, and presentation copies of books and odd souvenirs, many from the theater. A fire of cannel coal glowed in the open grate when Beach presented himself promptly at eleven o'clock. Marion led him to a big chair at the hearth and poured tea for him. She had changed her pert street costume for a simple house dress that fell straight from her shoulders. The neck was cut round and modestly high, and the general effect was to make her seem even younger; a little girl playing "grown up."

For some time she talked at random, and Beach listened, willing to await her business and amused by her chatter. She glanced at a clock nervously, saw it was late, and hesitated.

"Did forgetting about your problem help you to think it out straight?" Beach prompted helpfully.

"I made up my mind, anyhow. I'm going to talk business to you now. Will you consider what I say seriously—as a business proposition?"

Beach nodded. He looked particularly handsome and amiable and helpful. She thought how little effort it meant for him to do the thing she wished, and gained courage.

"I want to talk to you about this Hayes affair. In confidence, of course."

"I don't know much about this Hayes affair," Beach said quickly. "I make it my business not to. Can't you and Fox—"

"Fox can't settle what I have in mind. In fact, Fox is the last man in the world who must know of it. Do you like Hayes?"

Beach considered the abrupt question. "If you mean as an acquaintance, I think he's a decent sort. Rather admire him, in fact—"

"You believe he is honest, don't you?"

"Absolutely, ridiculously, primitively honest. Yes!"

"And if he says he knows where there are a lot of sealskins, they are there? You don't think he'd lie about that?"

"No. I think the skins are where he says. Already told Fox I thought that."

"Fox doesn't believe it," Marion said earnestly. "Fox doesn't even want to believe. He wants to exploit this scheme for the easy money in it, and that's all he cares about. And I say that's giving Hayes a pretty dirty deal."

Beach looked surprised at her vehemence—surprised and rather suspicious. If he had been critical he might have reminded the girl that she was the one who was responsible for the deal Hayes was getting. He diplomatically avoided that issue.

"It is rather rough on the cave man," he agreed. "But just what had you thought of doing about it?"

"I thought of doing this." Marion was serious and business-like as she leaned toward him. "I'd like to see Hayes shake Fox and all Fox's schemes and go get those skins for himself—decently and honestly. They're his. He deserves the chance. What I suggest is that you give him that chance."

"I?"

"You. Why not? You have money."

"Well!" Beach cried half humorously. "Here, hold on! Maybe the reason I have money is because I don't invest in things like that!"

"My dear friend, that's all bunk, and you know it. It doesn't cost so much to outfit Hayes with a ship and let him get these sealskins. Your investment and your profit can be absolutely guaranteed. Why, just Hayes's word is good for that! Considered as a business proposition, there is nothing the matter with it—and I'm asking you to go into it. Give Hayes his chance."

Beach stopped smiling. A look of thoughtful calculation had come into his gray eyes. "Do you know what you're asking? You want me to invest a lot of money in a risky chance—a romantic adventure. And not only that—you want me to incur the undying dislike of Douglas Fox, who is an amusing chap if he is crude; also he's my friend. You want me to double-cross him and spoil his pet scheme."

"I want you to give Hayes his chance," Marion repeated. "If Fox suffers—if he is double-crossed—his conduct has invited all that's coming to him. Give Hayes a chance."

"Why?" Beach asked coldly.

"Because he deserves it."

"Again, why?"

"Because you can make money out of it."

He shrugged. "I don't need money. Any other reason?"

"Because I ask you to."

Marion looked up at him appealingly. She managed a wistful smile with the words and her fingers touched the lapel of Beach's coat coaxingly. He returned the look with evidence of due appreciation for her pretty pleading, but plainly he was not won over.

"I thought you wouldn't mind doing a little thing like that—for me," Marion murmured.

Such a look as she gave him, and such words and inflection of tone, had been effective many times. Marion saw that this time they failed to get the desired result. Beach was different metal, more unyielding metal than any she had tried. Beach was used to having his own way if he happened to want it badly enough.

The sportsman captured the fingers that were touching his coat lapel and returned the hand to Marion's knee, as if he realized that her touch was a little too persuasive for good judgment.

"I'm going to return your question of a few minutes ago," he said. "Do you like Hayes?"

She shrugged. "Would I go to all this trouble if I didn't?"

"But just how much do you like him?"

"Well, really, Beach—"

"Marion, if you ever went to a bank to borrow money on a business proposition, you understand how they question you and why. I'm questioning you for just the same purpose. You bring me a business proposition, and I'm trying to find out—just like the banker—what there is in it for me? Do you understand?"

Marion began to protest, falling back on dignity. "I know what you're getting at! You're going to put this on personal grounds. You want to make a trade, don't you? It's going to simmer down to personal relations—Hayes and you—and me."

"Excuse me if I remind you that it was you who put this on personal grounds," Beach argued gently. "You made a very pretty plea, purely on personal grounds. Oh, I know! Other pretty ladies have asked favors of me in that way. That moist eye and trembling lip and implied promise! I have been moved to do favors before this through such dainty pantomime—and when the promises were performed, my dear, the pretty ladies scornfully disclaimed any intention or suggestion that they would do anything in return. You chose the personal grounds, Marion—I'm only trying to reduce the bargain to plain terms. If there's anything in it for me I want to know it. Brutal? Yes, but businesslike. Now, do you love Hayes?"

"Silly question! No, I do not. But I'm sorry for the poor fish—and I would like to see him get a square deal."

"Then, just how grateful would you be to me if I saw to it that he does get a square deal?"

"What do you mean by that?"

"About what it seems to mean. You know how crazy I am about you. You know how I've been trying to make you listen to me. You are very skillful in evading issues of that sort, my dear. So I'm trying to put this in words that can't be evaded. In plain English, I'm willing to help Hayes—if you are willing to marry me."

Beach delivered this ultimatum calmly enough, but he added with passion: "You know I love you! I want you worse than I ever wanted any woman. It was something I thought for a long time might wear off—or could be put aside. But it isn't that sort at all. Marion, there's just one way in the world you can make me happy, and that's by your promise to marry me."

Marion had risen and looked white and angry. Her small figure was tense. She said, a little more slowly than her wont and in a voice that was hoarse: "And you think I would trade in things like that! Beach, I didn't know you were—yellow."

Beach also rose and faced her calmly. Quick, hot resentment flashed in his gray eyes, but he answered coolly:

"I remind you again that trading was your initiative. I merely clarified your diplomacy. There seems to be nothing more to say—"

"There is nothing more to say."

"Yes—one thing." He paused on his way toward the door. "What I said about loving you—I mean. I shall always love you—always."

Marion managed a bitter smile. "Thank you—for the perfect insult."

When the door had closed behind him she was shaking with a nervous chill. She flung herself into a chair—presently she knew that somebody was crying hysterically. It was herself—Marion Reade!

Yet a month or two ago she had planned and worked deliberately to win Beach—scheming shrewdly for his proposal to marry her! Even now the sophisticated, scheming side of her couldn't understand why she felt like this.

Hayes and Al Sapley were walking. They had followed the almost nightly program of Broadway amusement; but after the theater the Alaskan refused any more of Broadway.

"Not tonight," he declared. "I'm too nervous—too restless. I'm sick of hot rooms and the smell of perfumes and food. Sick of braying orchestras. I want some quiet and fresh air, some place where you can see stars instead of electric lights."

Sapley agreed with a stifled sigh. He hated walking.

"What's a taxi for?" he wanted to know. "If you've got to have exercise we could have the boy drive us around the park."

"If you're going with me you'll walk," Hayes said grimly.

"Yours for broken arches!" Sapley grinned, making the best of it.

They crossed Forty-Second Street to Fifth Avenue, and started toward the park. For a time they wandered there, then Hayes struck back into the avenue again, heading south. He took a long, space eating stride, not so very fast but deadly effective. Sapley had little breath to talk and Hayes said nothing at all. The wide, silent, almost deserted street and glimpses of the starry night sky comforted him—and he had need of comfort.

Cook's words were a slow, subtle poison that spread and gained in potency. They colored most of his thoughts, in spite of all he could do to forget them. He had said truly that Marion's world had him wondering. That uncertainty, the suspicion he could not down, gave Hayes need of all the philosophy and courage he could summon. He turned instinctively to the open air for counsel.

He was aware that Sapley was protesting. "Listen, sucker, my dogs hurt something awful! You don't want to cripple me permanently, do you? And I'm hungry. Let's find a one-arm lunch and forget this fresh air stuff for a minute. There ought to be something on Fourteenth."

Hayes agreed. But before they reached Fourteenth Street Sapley had another idea. "There's Marion's studio, and her light's burning. We'll stop there before you have to page an ambulance for me!" He led Hayes, slightly protesting, around the corner into Sixteenth Street. "Oh, Lord," he groaned, "feet! How I hate 'em—my own especially. Any time anybody gets me to do another O'Sullivan—"

Al stopped short and his fingers tightened on Hayes's arm. He drew Hayes back into the shadow and they saw Beach coming out of the studio-building entrance.

Beach walked briskly into Fifth Avenue and disappeared, unaware of the espionage.

Al Sapley whistled long and low. "So that's that!" he exclaimed, rather staggered.

"What are you talking about?" Hayes growled suspiciously.

"Beach—Marion—2 a.m. of a fine, frosty night—everything, that's all!"

"What of it?"

"If you had any eyes in your head you'd know what of it! Beach is worth a heap of jack. Every show girl on Broadway knows that, and most of 'em have tried to knick that roll of his. Some have succeeded. Marion Reade's been scheming and working all summer to land Beach, and now it looks as if she'd got somewheres."

"Are you suggesting," Hayes asked steadily, "that Marion is going to marry Beach?"

"Marry him!" Al glanced sharply at the Alaskan. He caught

his arm. "Sucker, get wise!" he exclaimed. "I'm telling you for your own good. Beach is a hard-boiled bird—and he's not the marrying kind. Marion knows that as well as anybody, and the girl's no fool. She can watch her own step, thank you! If this is what I think it is, she'll get something pretty out of it—"

Al Sapley's words ended in a screech that strangled in his throat. Hayes had caught him round the neck and hurled him savagely against the house wall behind them. Sapley went to his knees and the big Alaskan picked him up by the collar as if he were a sack stuffed with paper.

"You—dirty—hound!" Hayes's expression was murderous.

Sapley was clawing the air. "For God's sake—oh, for God's sake!" he protested. "What'd I do? What—"

"You insulted the name of a decent woman. Now you will—"

"I never meant to. I—listen, sucker, how did I know she was—that you felt that way—about her? I never guessed. I'm sorry, I tell you. I apologize—"

"Yes, you will apologize," Hayes declared, shaking him. "You'll apologize—to her!"

"I tell you I'm sorry. Lay off me—"

"You can tell that to Marion."

Al gasped and squeaked with new terror. "What d'you mean?"

"I mean you are going up there with me and make your apology where it is due—"

"Have a heart! I apologize, don't I? I'm asking your pardon. What's the use bothering Marion—"

"You insulted Marion—a decent girl. You said the foulest thing a man can say about a woman. And you're going to answer—before her." Hayes's face was hard as granite. He began to drag the helpless Sapley across the street toward the studio.

Sapley fought wildly. "Listen to reason," he pleaded. "Can't you listen to a little reason! You don't want this to go any farther. Hayes—think what you're doing—Hayes!"

But Hayes marched on, and Sapley went with him, protest-ing in vain, struggling vainly against a giant's strength.

Hayes found Marion's bell and rang it; the street door latch clicked. He pushed in and dragged his victim upstairs and along corridors until he found the studio door. Sapley had ceased to argue now. He was dumb and he went without a struggle, but there was a look growing in his eyes that was not only shame and humiliation, but something harder.

Marion opened her door to Hayes's knock and stared aghast at the spectacle the two men made.

Hayes pushed in and announced grimly: "This man has something to say to you. Now, Sapley, tell her what you said and apologize."

In a sort of savage desperation Sapley protested once more. "No, damn you! You can kill me, but you can't make me do that. You—"

The big hand twisted his collar and choked off his words. Hayes held him thus for a moment, then released him sud-denly. "Talk," he ordered.

Sapley's face, purpling with congested blood, faded to a sickly white. His eyes fixed their gaze on a crack in the floor as he repeated like some new and strange automaton, "I said exactly what everybody's been saying since last summer, that you made a play for Beach and you went into it with your eyes open. I said you were wise to Beach and his other affairs, and if you were after that bird it was because of the jack that's in it and—and not because you expected to marry him—"

"And now!" Hayes prompted.

"Now, I got to say I'm sorry I said it. And I apologize to you." Sapley added with a rush of anger, "That's every damn word I'm going to say. Before I'm done I'll make you damn sick of this night, you big hick!"

Hayes took him by the shoulder, opened the door and put him into the hall. "Get out," he said.

He closed the door again and stood facing the utterly astounded woman. Hayes's mouth was grim and his eyes were hard. He had some difficulty controlling his breathing as he faced Marion. It was a little unsteadily that he announced, "I have something to say to you now. You will please listen."

CHAPTER XV

THE BITTER TRUTH

OUT OF THE bewilderment and confusion of Hayes's tempestuous entrance at such an hour and Sapley's revelation and apology, Marion Reade realized one thing very clearly as she faced the big Alaskan: that he was about to say something she must not let him say.

It was not the time to let Hayes talk. The man was overwrought with horror and anger at Sapley—perhaps at Beach, too. He would say things they each would regret. She knew it—and if Hayes began that way Marion couldn't answer for her own self-control.

She took Hayes by the arm. "No talk tonight—please. Tomorrow I'll listen to anything you have to say—"

"You will listen tonight."

"Hayes, be reasonable! Not here, at this hour—"

"You will listen to me!"

"I ask you as a favor, don't—don't say anything—not tonight! Hayes, I beg of you—"

"You will listen to me tonight."

His stubborn reiteration was maddening. She flared out, "*Will* listen? *Will*, you say? Who are you to order what I shall do? This is my home. I'm living my own life. I'll order my own affairs. Do you think you can break in here like a hoodlum at two o'clock in the morning and get away with it? Now, you—you can get out!"

She reached past him and flung open the door. "Follow your friend, Al Sapley," she said bitterly.

Hayes caught her arm with a heavy hand and released it from the knob. He put her aside gently and closed the door. "Sit down. It's time you learned a few things that any woman of sense would have known years ago. Do you know what kind of fool you've been making of yourself? Do you realize now?"

Astonishment and indignation choked her. She gasped. "Do you know what you're saying—and who you're saying it to?"

"Yes. I'm saying it to you. You've made a fool of yourself. You've played that woman's game of yours once too often—and you picked the wrong man in Beach. You—who thought you were so clever—do you know what you've done? You've made your name and reputation the latest Broadway joke. You've heard what Sapley said. He's right. That's what they all say. I'm here to warn you to be careful—"

"You! Warn me? What right have you? And where, pray, did you get the mad idea that anything you said would have any effect?"

Marion was wonderful in her indignation. Her scorn of him—the anger that carried away her more sober judgment, made her like a flame—bright, beautiful and dangerous.

"Answer me"—she was majestic—"who gave you any right? Where do you get the idea you can come here and say things like that to me?"

Hayes said sternly, "I say that because I love you."

"You love me!"

"I do love you."

She laughed and the effect of that musical, chiming laugh was startling. Rage had made a wonderful actress of the girl. She laughed at his love with such light-heartedness that it disconcerted him.

"I do love you," he repeated. "Laugh all you please; you can't change it. And because I love you I'm warning you that you're throwing away everything worthwhile. Because of Beach you

are endangering your good name. You have let him make a fool
of you—"

"A fool! So, I'm a fool, am I? I? Good God, and I let *you*
stand there and tell me that!"

This was too much. The man she had pitied and tried to
protect and help, saying a thing like that. The man she had been
bargaining for with Beach, telling her these things! Jonathan
Hayes of Kalvik Island, of all people in the world, calling her
a fool!

She was too angry now to care for any consequences. There
seemed but one thing in the world worth doing, that was to
prick the bubble of this colossal conceit—to hurt this man—this
hick—this supreme dumb-bell who had dared what no other
man ever dared—to call her a fool.

She pointed a scornful finger at him and began to speak,
slowly at first, every word clear cut and thrilling with her contemptuous laughter.

"Speaking of fools, I want you to listen to me. I'm going to
try to get a little truth into that thick Alaskan skull of yours,
Jonathan Hayes. Every word of it is true and without exaggeration. Heaven knows it needs no exaggeration!

"Do you want to know who is the fool, who is the joke of
Broadway, the hottest laugh that was ever handed this town?
You are, my hick friend!

"Do you want to know who was captured in his native lair
and dragged out to civilization like a dancing bear on a chain
for the amusement of a cheap sucker crowd and the profit of
Douglas Fox? You were!

"Do you want to know whom Fox and Ada and Beach and
Sapley—and everybody who knows about it or can make a good
guess—considers the funniest sketch and the biggest simpleton
civilization has discovered? That's you.

"A fool—that's you. Easy pickings—that's you! The man who
didn't know any better than to let Douglas Fox, the promoter

of more swindles than any man on Broadway, use him for sucker bait. You again!

"And who brought you here? Who led you around on a leash? Who made a tame cave man out of you, warranted not to scratch, bite, or even think for himself? I did! And you call me a fool!"

She laughed again, and the music of her tinkling laugh was perfect.

"You call me a fool!" she repeated. "You! You! Oh, that is rich!"

She stopped laughing with a sudden catch of the breath when she saw Hayes's face. He had gone red, then white. Now there was something queer and quiet about him that frightened Marion. There had been something of that look the night on Kalvik when she shirked sentry duty against Cook's men; again when he kissed her and damned her in the same breath, and again when he said he loved her—something of this look each of these times, but never so marked as now.

The hysterical anger that had goaded her into saying things she had no intention of saying just for the inhuman joy of hurting this man who had the power to hurt her, evaporated. She looked at Hayes and she was afraid.

Hayes said quietly, almost musingly, "Cook was right! I was afraid of that. And you are right—quite right. I am the bigger fool of the two of us." He turned to the door.

Marion whispered shakily, "Where are you going?"

"I don't know—why, yes! To the hotel—to bed."

"But—but—no! You're going to do something! Hayes, I can see it in your eye! You're going to do something—"

She caught his sleeve. "Be careful," she whispered. "Oh, be careful. Don't—don't do anything!"

He looked at her a little vaguely. "All right," he agreed. "Not tonight. When I do, I'll let you know."

"You promise me that? You promise!"

"I promise."

He opened the door and went away.

She was left facing that screen of hardwood paneling that eliminated him from the room. Her hand clawed at her mouth with a terrible gesture of futility. She was whispering to herself, "I've done it—I have done it this time! Dear God, what a ghastly mess!"

CHAPTER XVI

KALVIK ISLAND JUSTICE

MARION GOT TO Fox's office early next morning before Fox. She had not slept at all. She wanted to warn Fox, had made up her mind that she must warn Fox—and yet she had no liking for that interview.

It would not be pleasant to tell Fox that she had wrecked his pet scheme, but the blame was hers and she could not deny it. Fox must be told. There was no getting away from that. He must be warned before Hayes did anything—anything wild and desperate.

She had tried several times, and vainly, to reach Hayes by the telephone. Either he had never gone to his hotel or would answer no calls. She was almost afraid to go back to that office.

But the office was cheerful and commonplace when she came in. The stenographers were at work and an office boy nodded a smiling good morning. "Couple reporters waiting in the reception room, Miss Reade." Marion wondered if by any chance she had dreamed the events of the last few hours. Already they were far away and vague in outline. But she knew there was no such good luck as that.

She stopped in the reception room to speak to the newspaper men. There were three of them from evening papers, and another came in as she was talking. They gathered around her.

"What's doing with the Eskimo millionaire today?" they wanted to know.

Marion shrugged her shoulders and smiled. "Not a thing that I know of, boys. But I'm obliged to you for asking."

"Well, there's something! All the city desks in town got a tip there'd be a story here. When's it going to happen?"

"Honestly, I don't know," Marion said truthfully. "Probably Mr. Fox has some statement to issue. He'll be in shortly." She excused herself and went to Fox's office to wait his coming.

The promoter arrived soon after her. Fox was smiling and breezy. "This morning's ads look immense!" he exclaimed. "The girl says the first mail brought a couple inquiries for stock. Didn't I tell you suckers were ripe to bite?"

Fox eyed her curiously. "You're working too hard," he decided gruffly. "Don't kill yourself on this job. The hard work's all over, anyhow. Nothing to do now but count the gate receipts. Why don't you take the weekend and go down to Atlantic City? And, oh, yes, what are all these reporters waiting for?"

Marion exclaimed, "I thought you sent for them? I didn't."

"No, I didn't. What's the big idea, I ponder—"

"They said every paper in town had a tip to get a man up here for a good story."

"Well," Fox exclaimed, "somebody has pulled a boner! No story here—unless they want to print something about how the stock is selling—"

"Don't try to hand them that bunk!"

"I won't. I'll pass the cigars and say it was a mistake—"

"Then I must talk to you—about something serious," Marion exclaimed.

"Be right with you as soon as I give these reporters the gate—" Fox paused in the doorway and exclaimed, "Oh, hello Hayes! Looking for me?"

Marion was conscious of a sudden giddiness. There was something cold in her breast where her heart had been. She held to the back of a chair to keep her balance.

"I am looking for you," Hayes answered. She noticed that he

spoke with slow and careful deliberation, as a man would speak whose tongue was slightly fuddled by liquor. "Is Marion here?"

"Sure. Inside—"

"That's good, very good," Hayes went on with that queer, precise way." Fox backed into the room and the Alaskan followed him. Not alone was his voice peculiar, but his manner. At another time she would have laughed, for Hayes was exactly like a man humorously bewildered by alcohol. He bore himself with the same stiffness, the same restraint, the same fumbling attempt to keep himself under control.

This morning, if there was any humor in Hayes's appearance it was grim. To Marion he seemed more terrible than a man in a towering rage, for she guessed that he was fighting with all his strength to keep a towering rage subdued—to control himself.

Fox noticed Hayes's peculiarity and evidently set it down to the obvious explanation of alcohol. He flashed an amused side glance at Marion, expressive of surprise and raillery. It seemed to say, "Well! Look who's here. A cave man with a souse!"

To Hayes Fox spoke jovially. "Sit down, Old Timer! Take a load off your feet. You're in the hands of your friends."

Marion's hand went to her lips in terror at these last ill-chosen words. She wanted to scream a warning to Fox, to tell him he was playing with dynamite, but she was too frightened to do it.

Hayes sat down, fumblingly, as he did everything this morning. "You—sit down," he said to Fox gravely.

Fox laughed again, to cover his own surmises. "Have a cigar—or a little drink? Anything you want in the safe—"

"No. I want to talk to you, Fox. I want to talk about business—"

Marion rose hastily. "Then I'll be going—"

"Wait!" Hayes said it quietly, but the word stopped her like a shot. "You stay. Here. Now Fox—" He hesitated and shivered.

He passed his hand before his eyes, bewildered by this intoxication of anger.

Marion was aware that Fox was slyly kicking her foot under the table and winking broadly. Fox was enjoying what he conceived to be a very funny joke. She could stand it no longer.

"Fox!" she exclaimed.

Hayes raised his hand. "Wait," he said thickly. "I will try to explain things in my own way. Let me talk."

"Sure you won't have another drink?" Fox expressed. "All right. Talk away, Old Timer."

"Yes," Hayes said, "I will talk. I—" He leaned across the table, his face close to Fox's, looking at Fox eye to eye. "You played me—for a—sucker, didn't you, Fox?"

"Who, me? Why Hayes, what's eating you!"

"You made a fool of me—a sort of dancing bear to advertise your swindle. That's it, isn't it?"

Fox struck a dramatic posture, expressive of horror. "Hayes! My God, what is eating you today? Why, Hayes—"

Hayes pressed on: "It was a swindle, wasn't it? You didn't care about the sealskins. You didn't care a damn about anything but the stock you could sell. You were using me just to bait your trap, and the thing you care about least of all is what happens to me—what happens to my good name. When you finished using me you meant to kick me aside—like an old shoe—isn't that right?"

Fox had gone very red. He blustered loudly, smacking the table with his fist and raising his voice to a roar. "Stop! Stop right where you are! You can't talk to me—"

"Fox! Fox, *if you value your life* don't shout at me. Don't do it."

Fox must have seen then that there was murder seething in Hayes's heart. He shrank back in his chair, his bluish eyes round and glassy. A twitching seized his full lower lip. He forgot what he meant to say and abandoned all idea of saying it.

"I want you to tell the truth this morning, Fox; nothing else.

Is it true, as I have said, that you were using me to advertise your stock swindle?"

"It isn't a swindle. You can't prove that—"

"Fox! Answer the question."

"Yes. I used you—"

"You do not believe in these sealskins? You never expected to get them—or looked for dividends from them? Is that true?"

"I—you can't prove a word of it—"

"Answer the question."

"I—yes, damn you!"

"And the whole thing is a swindle, a swindle on me and on the public?"

"Who says—"

"Answer!"

"Say, listen here—"

Marion clutched at Fox's arm. "In Heaven's name answer him," she warned. "Tell the truth if you value your life!" Fox bowed his head.

"In words," Hayes prompted. "Say it!"

"It was—a—swindle."

Hayes looked at Marion. "You are witness to all this," he reminded her, and rising, went to the door that communicated with the reception room where the wondering newspaper men waited. "Please come in this room, gentlemen," he invited.

The reporters came and formed an awkward little group. It did not need the trained instinct of a reporter to guess that something had been happening among these three. Fox was pasty white, collapsed in his chair, staring fixedly at the opposite wall and breathing hard. Marion huddled in a chair near by, her hand at her lips. Hayes towered above them all, and his obvious effort to control himself made them shrink from him.

Hayes went to the several communicating doors, turned their locks and dropped the keys in his pocket. The newspaper men murmured uneasily.

"Let me tell you something," Hayes said sternly. "Before we go any further, let me warn you all. Don't interfere! Anybody who tries to stop me in what I am going to do is going to get hurt."

Fox sprang to his feet in a panic, but Hayes's pointing finger dropped him as if it had been a bullet.

"Stay right where you are!" Hayes commanded. He turned to the newspaper men.

"I asked you gentlemen to come here this morning. Since I have been in your city you have printed a good deal about me—and about Kalvik Island. I'm going to ask you to print one thing more in your newspapers. I want you to tell your readers about Kalvik Island justice."

Fox's hand was stealing across the table, reaching for the telephone.

Marion stopped him with an exclamation. "Don't! Don't do that! Don't touch that button, either! Don't do anything, if you put any value on your life."

"No," Hayes repeated, "don't do it, Fox." He turned again to the newspaper men.

"You know this man, Douglas Fox? He is a promoter. Last summer he came to the island where I have lived, and when he heard that I knew the location of some valuable pelts he made a contract with me, by which he was to form a company to find and sell the skins. I agreed to come with him to this city. I was ignorant, absolutely ignorant, innocent of your civilization and all its ways. What this man—and his associates—told me to do, I did. I was like a child in their hands, and like a child, I trusted everything to them. Everything. I dressed when they told me to dress, and in the clothes they told me to wear. I ate when they told me. I slept when they told me to sleep. The things I have done and the things I have said are the things this man has told me to do and say, the things he advised me were right and proper to help him in his plan of helping me— things he told me were honorable, honest things. Morning, noon and night, waking and sleeping, I have been a child in this man's hands, clay that he could mold to suit himself.

"This morning, just now, Douglas Fox has admitted before this witness, that his scheme is a deliberate swindle. That his whole intention was to sell stock, using all this publicity he got through me to attract his gulls. He confesses he is a swindler and a cheat, and he has degraded me to help out his crooked purpose." Hayes swung on Fox suddenly. "Is this true? Answer!"

Fox rolled his eyes at them all and his lips twitched, but seemed incapable of speech.

Marion spoke, and so unexpectedly they all started. "It is true. I heard Fox admit it."

"You know it is true—of your own knowledge," Hayes said bitterly.

"*Yes.* I know it is true—of my own knowledge."

Hayes strode over to Fox's chair. "Fox, stand up!"

The promoter hesitated and Hayes pulled him from the chair and away from the table where he faced him. "Put up your fists," he said, hoarsely. "Defend yourself."

Fox found his voice. "For God's sake—somebody! Are you all going to stand and see murder done?"

Hayes jerked a glance at his audience. "Remember," he warned, "anybody who interferes will get hurt. Now, Fox!"

Fox backed slowly toward the table. He made no attempt to raise his fists. In a moment he was pressed tightly against the table edge. Although there was several feet between him and Hayes he acted as if the man's nearness was enough to flatten his body against that furniture.

"Defend yourself!" Hayes growled.

Fox suddenly pulled open a drawer of the table. His hand sought and found a pistol, and almost instantly discharged it at Hayes. The noise was deafening.

Fox's aim was poor.

The report was followed by the scuffling of the two men, a

scream from Fox and the crash of a plate glass window breaking as Hayes hurled the pistol through it. The blow of Hayes's fist started Fox spinning, and a second blow halted him almost as quickly.

Fox, driven to it, hurled himself at the Alaskan and landed a smashing blow of his own. A moment they were intertwined, clinching, and then the sharp *smack-smack* of fists on flesh that sent Fox half way across the big room where he collapsed like a sack.

Hayes followed him up and examined him grimly.

"The man is not dead," he announced. "I was careful of that. Probably he is not even permanently disfigured, but I pray God I have put a scar on his soul that will make him loathe himself until the day he dies."

Hayes went to the outer door of the office and unlocked it. He threw it open, pressed through the group of terrified office assistants and disappeared.

Marion was first to break the silence that held them. "Splendid!" she cried, "he's splendid! Every word he said was the truth. Everything he did was right! I love him for it!"

CHAPTER XVII

"YOU CAN'T QUIT NOW!"

MARION HUNTED FOR three days before she found Jonathan Hayes. He disappeared completely when he walked out of Douglas Fox's office and left Fox bruised and scarred to wake to consciousness that only made him wish he could forget.

The hotel knew nothing of Hayes's plans. He was gone, and the only souvenir of him was the remnant of the store of spectacular souvenirs Douglas Fox had bought for distribution by the "Eskimo Prince." There was no value in the lot of it.

In her search for Hayes Marion encountered Al Sapley and asked his help.

"Don't know where he is," Sapley said briefly. "Don't want to know. All I got to say is don't let me know when you find him. If I see him there's going to be a shooting."

She saw that Sapley was in earnest and wondered. "Al, you saw the papers? You heard what Hayes did?"

"Not being deaf, dumb or blind, I did! You can't hear anything else around this town—"

"But isn't he splendid? Oh, Al! Isn't he splendid!"

Al stared at her with bitter scorn. "*So* you're falling for this rough stuff, are you? Splendid! That's your idea of splendid, is it? A big roughneck beating somebody up—walking over men because he packs a bigger punch than they do. Splendid? Hell!"

"But he did right. He did absolutely the one thing he could do. He gave Fox exactly what was coming to him, and in the most effective way. You've got to admire that—"

"Fox! Oh, I don't give a damn about Fox. But for what he did to me—"

Marion said dryly: "You had it coming to you, too!"

"I didn't have it coming to me that anybody should rub my face in the dirt! Apologize? Yes. But treat me like I was some kind of poodle, make me grovel? I want to tell you right now, no man's going to do that and get away with it if he leaves me alive. Get that!"

There was a venom in Al's bitterness that made Marion wonder. She knew that Al Sapley was a bad man to cross.

Al laughed his way through most of life, his being a sophisticated sort of laughter. In a gathering he was usually the willing clown. If you were his friend he cheerfully admitted that he lived by his wits and his lack of conscience. But back of all this Al had his sense of dignity. Hayes cut him deeply when he dragged him before Marion to apologize. Marion hadn't had time to think about Al in the rush of other events—but found herself wishing, now, that Hayes had not made such an enemy.

Marion was not the only person in New York who was seeking Jonathan Hayes of Kalvik. Every newspaper had men looking for him. The latest exploit of the man who bought Broadway was sensational enough to whet public appetite for more. It needed a follow-up. Douglas Fox was in a hospital and refused to say anything. Hayes must be found and made to talk or the newspapers were left with nothing to do except repeat vague rumors and retell the things that had already happened. It was a newspaper reporter who brought word of Hayes's discovery to Marion.

"He's in a Mills hotel," the newspaperman said. "It's he. He admits that. But when I said I was a newspaperman and asked him about Fox I thought he was going to throw me through a window! My gosh, Miss Reade, I don't mind taking chances! I take lots of chances. But I'm not stuck on locking myself in a cage with a bear that's got a sore head. Jumping under a subway train is so much quicker!"

"Perhaps he doesn't want to talk for publication." Marion smiled.

"Say! You know that occurred to me, too!" The reporter grinned sarcastically. "But how much good would it do me to tell that to my boss? Now, you're a friend of Hayes. You can handle him. I thought we might make a deal on this. I'll take you to him and you get him to say something for the paper. An exclusive interview, you know. Will you do that?"

"I can't promise results, but I'll try." How different from this day last week, or any time before, when she could promise offhand that Hayes would do whatever she chose! Strangely enough Marion was prouder of her uncertainty than she had been of her complete mastery of the man.

It was a note from Marion, delivered by the reporter, that brought Hayes from the hotel of frugal living to the street corner where Marion waited in a taxi. "I must talk to you," she exclaimed. "Will you ride up to the park with me?"

Hayes seemed strangely apathetic. "Whatever you say," he agreed and got in the cab.

Marion hesitated a little fearfully. "I promised Mr. Small of the *Planet* I would ask you to give him an interview. I had to do that to find you at all! Do you—mind?"

"Anything you wish. If you promised that we must keep your promise."

The reporter rode uptown with them, asking questions. With Marion's help, tactfully offered, Hayes made a statement that confined itself to things which had happened. But it was an interview, an exclusive interview, and Small considered himself richly paid for his trouble.

Dismissing the reporter, Marion glowed with pride. That meager interview, extracted from Hayes, seemed to her an achievement. "Let's get rid of this taxi," she suggested. "I want to talk business to you."

For a time they walked and said little. Hayes was gravely attentive to her. He answered questions, but volunteered nothing. Something in the man was dead. He lacked spirit. Marion could not understand what had happened to him. He inspired in her an overwhelming sense of pity and desire to help. Finally, when they were sitting in an isolated little summer house overlooking the lake, now bleak and wintery, she asked point-blank: "Hayes, you have got to tell me what ails you?"

"What ails me?"

"Yes! Something's wrong. What's happened to you?"

At least she stirred a spark of resentment in him. "That's a funny question—coming from you!" he exclaimed bitterly.

"I don't think it's funny at all! What's the matter with you? What's got into you? What do you mean by running away and hiding? Don't you know I've been looking everywhere for you— and all the newspapers were looking?"

"Good God! Do you think I wanted to talk to newspaper-men? Do you think I wanted to see anybody—even you? Do you think I am proud of my disgrace—and want to flaunt it?"

"Disgrace! You're not in disgrace. What are you talking about?"

"Not disgraced? When all the world knows I was partner in that crooked scheme of Fox's. When everybody knows me for his partner—a swindler's partner—a swindler myself!"

Marion laughed a little hysterically. "Have you read the newspapers?" she demanded.

"No," he groaned, "and don't want to."

She laughed harder. "Why, you poor fish! Oh, Hayes, Hayes, you poor, innocent fish!"

Signs of bewilderment showed in Hayes's face.

Marion cried pityingly but shaken still by the hysterical impulse to laugh. "Why Hayes, you're a hero! You're a popular hero today—and you run away and hide because you think you're disgraced."

"What are you saying?"

"I'm telling you the newspapers have made a hero of you.

What you did to Douglas Fox is exactly what Douglas Fox has had coming to him for years—"

"Do they say that?"

Marion smiled. "Well, not exactly in print. Libel laws are still on the books. But the fact is generally known. It's one of those news items that travels by underground until it gets to the majority of opinion. And they call you the man who was honest enough to show up Fox even if it cost him all he had. They're all cheering you, because of the way you did it. Hayes, everybody loves a fight—and a fighting man. And if the man fights with some show of right on his side—if he does a thing like you did—why, he's the public's fair-haired boy and that's all there is to it! Wake up! You're a hero!"

"I don't understand it!" Hayes blinked at her with a surprise almost comical. "Now that people know the scheme was a swindle—"

"Bless your heart! They know you aren't a swindler. Sweet lady! Wait till you see some of the editorials. The one in yesterday's *Asterisk*, for instance: Big seven column head in black face, 'Kalvik Island Justice.' And a four-column cartoon and a column of speckle-faced bunk about crooked business men and the man who did the right thing—that's you!"

Hayes exclaimed happily, hopefully: "It's like that? Really?"

"You'll see for yourself."

He was silent for a few minutes and much shaken by her news. "That makes it easier—a lot easier," he said finally.

"Makes what easier?"

"My defeat."

"But, my dear man! You're not beat! I tell you you're a hero. Why, you've won—"

Hayes smiled wearily. "Won! I don't suppose you realize how amusing that sounds to me. Won! Won what?"

"It's something to win the good will of a few million people!"

"Not to me. That doesn't make up for what I lost—for my defeat. Yes, defeat! I tackled your civilization and it whipped me—whipped me first time—rolled me in the dirt. I thought I was big enough and shrewd enough to measure up to it—and it turned out I was a bigger fool than any of the moths."

"What?"

"Yes, a bigger fool! People may say I'm honest. Why shouldn't they? That's true. But I'm a fool—colossal—ridiculous in my sublime egotism—the poor, trusting dupe of a swindler like Douglas Fox. That hurts me. It hurts my pride. It hurts too deep to be forgotten. That's why I'm crawling back to Kalvik—"

Marion cried: "Wait! Did you say you were going back to Kalvik?"

"Naturally. What else could I do?"

"You're going to—quit?"

"I have quit."

"Hayes!"

Marion looked at him so aghast that the Alaskan began to defend himself.

"I tell you I am through! The public knows I'm a fool. I can't fight against that—haven't any fight left in me. Oh, I know! I've seen how this civilization of yours laughs at the man who's down. It's cruel. It's terrible. I—I haven't the courage to face that. I'm going home—" Marion cried: "You're not going back! You can't go back. You're going to go through with the thing. You're going to get those sealskins and make your fortune!"

"Make my fortune?" Hayes burst out, angrily. "Get that silly idea out of your head. A fortune! What in God's name do I want of a fortune?" He laughed harshly. "Did you think perhaps I wanted to dress up like an Eskimo again and give away more gold nuggets? Or perhaps you think I'd like to spend my money on show girls? Perhaps you think I'd prefer to make Broadway my permanent home? A fortune! If there's one thing I don't want, that's it!"

"You don't mean that. You don't understand. You can't condemn civilization because you've seen just that side of it.

You can do so many things with money—things you would like to do. You can help so many people—"

"No!" Hayes shook his head firmly. "You can't tempt me. There's nothing in the wide world can tempt me. All I ask of your world now is to be let alone. Let me go home!"

"You can't go home!"

"I can—and will—"

"No, you can't. Because you're not a quitter, Hayes. You've something left to do, something you will find is a lot more important than running back to Kalvik Island, when you understand. You're going to stick to this thing—fight it through— until you win those seal pelts—"

"What are you talking about?"

"I'm telling you that you don't dare quit!"

"And why don't I dare?"

"Because, Hayes, you can't afford to have the world think you a common liar and cheat."

"Who says such a thing?" Hayes growled.

"Everybody will say it, if you don't fight. The newspapers, the public, everywhere they'll put you down for another Douglas Fox—"

"But you told me that the papers—everybody—praised what I did!"

Marion addressed him with a grim determination. She beat time to her words with her small fist and her gaze held Hayes's attention riveted. "Get this straight! The newspapers are for you—now. Because they believe you're on the level. The minute they figure that you are not on the level—the minute they get a suspicion you might be like Fox—they'll be on your back like a wolf pack. And don't make any mistake about it, my friend, if you sneak back home to Kalvik Island they'll say things and print things about you that will be repeated even as far away as that. Even the Aleuts will hear about it!"

"But I don't understand—"

"Then you'd better understand! Do you think you can come here with all this talk about a fortune in sealskins—and kick up all the fuss you have—build up the reputation you have—and not deliver the goods? You cannot! Hayes, in all your life it was never so important that you show the world you are on the level about those sealskins, than right now. Either that or go down in history as a champion liar and welsher. And the only way you can show them is by *getting* those skins!"

Marion paused, a little breathless in her vehemence, and sank back on the rustic bench, watching Hayes's face. Her words showed one result, at least. The apathy had gone. The man was thinking with brows creased and his big hands were opening and closing their fingers nervously. Hayes slapped his knee.

"You're right; I can't quit now!"

"You must go through with it!"

"I will."

He looked up and about him with something of his old air, his calm confidence. Marion could have cried for joy at the change.

"You bet you will!" the girl repeated. "We'll get a ship. We'll go up there to Alaska and get those skins. We'll bring them back and tell all the world about them. Oh, Hayes, I'm proud of you!"

"It can be done," Hayes declared.

"It's going to be done!" Marion's hand gripped his tightly. She smiled back at him, but saw him only dimly, through a film of tears.

CHAPTER XVIII

HELP WANTED

HAYES CHECKED MARION'S enthusiasm with a strange look.

"How can I get those sealskins now? I have no money!"

Marion laughed, but not very naturally or happily. "That's good! I was overlooking that little thing altogether. Well, we must find the money."

"Find it?"

"Find somebody to lend it to us or finance the expedition. Will it need much?"

"To charter a ship and hire necessary men will need more than I ever saw," Hayes declared. "I haven't even carfare back to Kalvik—don't know how I would have got back there if I had carried out my threat. To be quite honest with you, I haven't enough to pay for another day's bed and board. I was at the end of the rope when you came."

Marion thought earnestly. "I have almost four thousand dollars in the bank. Would that do it?"

Hayes laughed. "That wouldn't even begin it. But God bless your generous heart for the offer!"

"Oh, well!" She tossed her head. "We'll find money. There's always somebody waiting to spend money on a gamble like that. Money is going to be the least of our worries!"

Hayes looked at her, so confident, so slender and beautiful in that soldierly, trig suit of tweed with the close-fitting hat of felt, her gold hair curling around its brim. She was so perfectly in accord with her time and environment that he did not doubt her.

"But there's one thing," Marion said earnestly. "You'll have to take a brace right away. I mean, you must quit that terrible hotel. Go back to a decent place. Not to spend the way Fox staged things, but to live decently, dress well, keep yourself full of good food so your heart will be full of courage. If you want something in this town, Hayes, you must go out after it looking as if you didn't *need* it. Remember, 'It's them that has, as gits.' If you're broke I'll stake you—no use frowning; this is absolutely necessary to our plans."

Once more Marion was giving orders and Hayes was obeying them. But there was a difference. The girl's orders had a new tone. Sometimes—often, in fact—they came as suggestions. She was slow in regaining the old confidence in her power. She would hesitate a long time before putting Jonathan Hayes over any hurdles!

Hayes established himself comfortably, as she suggested. He was careful to dress in the conservative good taste Marion advised. In all these details he followed orders explicitly.

He followed her orders, also, in taking his plan to various men who had money enough to back his expedition. Marion worked hard the next four weeks, using her wide acquaintance and pulling all her wires to find and visit all possible sources of backing.

But in one thing Marion guessed wrong. The public admired Jonathan Hayes and would for a few weeks until a newer hero came up; but nobody with money to invest had been impressed at all with the business merits of Hayes's fantastic treasure. Hayes met cordial receptions from curious, interested, sometimes sympathetic men of business, but when they learned he was seeking money to carry out his adventure; that he wanted to spend their money on the vague chance of finding more or less hypothetical sealskins stowed away under a glacier in an unknown bay in the almost equally unknown territory of Alaska, they chilled instantly. They were diplomatic, but they were all equally firm in saying no.

Marion carried the double burden of locating these sources of possible backing and cheering Hayes on to fresh interviews. Hayes was as determined as she, but when for a half dozen times he found all his simple, sincere eloquence slipping off the city businessman's smooth insulation without even scratching the surface, he became bewildered and downcast.

Marion herself was worse hit.

She had rushed into this partnership with Hayes on impulse. She meant to go through with it at any cost. She neglected all other interests in that hope without stopping to think where or to what it led. Continued reverses made her desperate. In that state of mind she encountered Beach one afternoon.

Beach bowed like a man a little uncertain about his reception, but he had no need to be. Marion, for the time, forgot all about their last interview. Her smile emboldened Beach to walk beside her. "And what are you doing since your wild man broke out of his cage?" he wanted to know.

"Starting a circus of my own."

"Not with the same wild man, surely?"

"The same." Marion looked up earnestly. "Beach, somebody in this town is going to help that big boob to get his sealskins and prove to the world he wasn't bluffing. Somebody has just got to do it! I don't know what it is—there's something sort of pitiful—and tragic about this chap Hayes—something that gets my goat! He's costing me a lot of time—and time means money to me. I have neglected my own work altogether these last few weeks. But I don't care! I'm going to put Hayes across."

Beach smiled warmly. "You're a good little sport!" he said. "But, Marion, is it fair—to Hayes—or to you? Are you sure you're right, fighting his battles for him?"

Marion stopped and her brown eyes flashed. "Right? Listen, Beach, get this straight! I got Hayes into this. He would never have gone on one step but for me. I got him in up to his neck—

worse than that; he was buried under the ruins when I found him. Now it strikes me it's up to me to get him out again!"

Beach looked at her with honest admiration. "I don't approve—not for a minute—but I can't help admiring your pluck. It's going to take a lot of courage—and luck—to put this over!"

She agreed so soberly that Beach smiled. "Evidently you haven't found a backer?"

"I have not."

"Tried pretty hard?"

"I've tried everything, and every one!" she burst out irritably. "Talk about a hard-boiled town! Talk about stupids! You can sell a gold brick to every second New Yorker you meet. Sure! Or you can take a tin can, cut a slot in the top and shake it in the subway, and nine out of every ten suckers will drop in a dime and never ask you why—or what you're going to do with the money! Wall Street bankers hire boys without references and trust them to carry a million dollars' worth of negotiable securities. When the boys drop out of sight with a million or so they seem only mildly surprised. But get any New Yorker to invest his money in a sure thing like Hayes? What a laugh! And why? Because he is the real thing; he is also honest, and nobody believes anything so real and honest can possibly be true. That's why!"

Beach smiled enviously. "I can see that you believe in him."

"You bet I do!"

She made a splendid little champion, her eyes flashing, her fists doubling belligerently. She was straight, slender, so very alive, so full of enthusiasm!

Beach sighed. "And if Hayes finds his fortune you'll marry him, I suppose?"

"Who says I will?"

"It seems the logical conclusion."

"Beach, you will mix sentiment with business!" she exclaimed. "Positively, you're mid-Victorian! Marry the poor boob? Why, in Heaven's name? Because I got him in a mess and am trying to help him out, must I necessarily close my act with the wedding march? Not in these times!"

Beach looked partly convinced by her eloquence. "This is strictly business. Really?"

"Strictly business. Why, Beach, it's only common humanity to give Hayes a hand when he's down and out like this. And he is down! The poor devil was all for slinking back home because he thought the world was laughing at him—thought he was a failure when, as a matter of fact, he did a pretty big thing in kicking over the traces. If we want to save his life— make it possible for him to face life with his chin up—we've got to give him this chance to show the world he isn't a four-flusher like Douglas Fox. He's got to produce those sealskins. Otherwise he'd be a lot better off—dead."

"There's a good deal in that," Beach acknowledged. "And you don't—don't contemplate anything more than that?"

"I have no more intention of marrying him than I had the day he came aboard the yacht, if that's what you mean—"

"Marion, you know I love you—"

"Oh, please, not in the middle of Forty-Second Street!"

"Yes, here and now!" Beach went on hurriedly. "The last time we talked about this I made you an offer. That offer is still open. If you are interested—"

"You mean that you are willing to furnish the money for this treasure hunt?"

"In exchange for your promise to marry me."

They walked in silence for a block. In the bright sunshine of this brisk winter day, with the eternal crowds streaming about them and the noise of traffic underground, on the surface, over-head, Marion felt that she must be dreaming. Beach's words repeated themselves over and over in memory, but their sub-stance, their thought was too absurd to be real. Was it possible she could consider them!

"Don't misunderstand me," Beach argued again. "If I were

asked to spend the money for you, my dear, there would be no string tied to it. For yourself you can have anything that I have without any obligation on your part. But when you ask me to spend my money on another man—a man in love with you—"

"Nonsense! He's not—"

"He is! And you're dangerously near loving him in return. When you ask a thing like that I'm jealous. If I spend one red cent to help Jonathan Hayes it's going to be because I expect to get my reward out of it—and that reward is you! What do you say?"

"I—I don't know."

Marion was in an agony of indecision. Getting Hayes the needed money had assumed an almost overwhelming importance in her thoughts. It seemed to her that his life depended on that, as she had explained to Beach. Her sense of responsibility for the Alaskan's predicament made her a little desperate.

Not very long ago she had turned on Beach angrily for his offer to trade. Today she heard it repeated, and her first emotion had been a great sense of relief that her search was ended!

Promise Beach? Why not! Last summer she had done her best to hook him as a matrimonial prize. She glanced appraisingly at him. A handsome chap. He had all the advantages of money and of moneyed ancestry. Something of a rounder, to be sure—a midnight son. She pretty thoroughly knew his past. She was bound to marry some day; why not promise Beach—and do Jonathan Hayes a real favor—a favor that would square the dirty trick she had played him?

What astonished her now was that she hesitated. Yet she did hesitate. "I—don't know."

"Then I tell you what you do," Beach suggested briskly. "Let me know within a week. I'll hold the proposition open. Just call me up—or drop me a line. Just say 'yes' and it will be all right with me. I know you don't welsh on your promises."

"Beach, if I should do that you wouldn't tell Hayes? He must not know—"

"That's hardly fair to the fellow, is it?"

"He simply must not know! I—I don't believe that he cares as much as he thinks he did—or anything like that—and I'm not so conceited that I think this would blight his life or anything of that sort. But—if Hayes knew about this—well, you see, he wouldn't go through with it, that's all. For his own sake it's got to be a secret—until I tell him myself."

"I agree to that, my dear. And your answer?"

"I'll let you know within the week. I—I've got to think it over. I've got to be sure, Beach!"

The next week was one of redoubled effort by Marion. She looked on it as a reprieve, a last minute chance to help out Hayes without making her bargain. She worked with frantic energy and made Hayes work. Time went by so rapidly she lost track of the days.

She sat in a restaurant with Hayes, a quiet little place on a side street, and realized with a start that her week was ended. They talked little during the meal. Both were beaten and realized it. It was hard to keep up the pretense of optimism. Over their coffee they sat in glum silence, Marion smoking and Hayes glowering at the tablecloth. She was astonished to hear Hayes break out with a chuckle: "Marion!" he exclaimed.

"Yes?"

"Marion! Of all the fools—of all the utter fools!"

"What—what's the matter?"

"Why, we forgot the one man in the world who can help me and might be persuaded. We forgot him completely!"

"What man? What possible chance have we forgot?"

Hayes cried exultantly, "Irving Beach!"

"Beach?" Her lips barely whispered the name. The blood stopped flowing in her veins. What freak of chance had put Beach's name into his mind?

Hayes was grinning happily. "The very man! Beach is square. He knows Alaska a little. I think he would believe in me. And I trust him—"

"I—I thought that you—hated—Beach!"

"Hate Beach? So I do. I hate him because of you. I hate him because you love him. If you were concerned in this, if it was a question of your happiness and your love I'd kill Beach, and enjoy doing it—"

"And yet you suggest asking Beach's help—"

"Because you are not concerned."

"Oh!" she whispered uneasily. "Oh—"

"This is between Beach and me and concerns only us. And if I hate Beach, because of you, I'm also willing to trust the man absolutely where I alone am concerned. That's my judgment of Beach—"

"You will see him? You're going to—ask—him—to help?"

"With your approval."

"My approval. I—"

"You are my partner in this," Hayes smiled. "Unless you tell me to do a thing, I refuse to go ahead. I rely on you—absolutely. Well, partner, shall I ask Beach?" Her lips formed a "Yes."

When she had said it there came the frantic desire to recall the word. But that would mean explanations. She dared not explain to Hayes—not now—when his future hung in the balance. The man was at the end of his rope, and she knew it. If he guessed what had passed between her and Beach he would never go on again. His success, which meant his honor, depended upon her secret. Her 'yes' could not be recalled!

"I'll see Beach tomorrow morning," Hayes announced with spirit.

"No, tonight. You must see him tonight!"

"It's pretty late! Why?"

"Because—" she lied without her usual skill. "Well, I met Beach on the street today—and he said—he was going out of town—tomorrow morning."

"Then I'll find him tonight. Right away." Hayes rose.

Marion fumbled through her small purse. She looked up eagerly. "Have you a nickel?"

Hayes laughed. "Of course. Here. Why that tragic look? You begged for that nickel as if your life depended on it. Don't squander it recklessly!"

"No, I won't. I'm just going—to the—telephone—a minute."

CHAPTER XIX

TWO BRAINY MEN

DOUGLAS FOX HAD been keeping to himself.

The promoter had several very good reasons for not desiring to be seen in public. A month of medical care and good surgery had not completely eliminated the reasons; the scars of Hayes's hard fists still disfigured Fox's face.

Fox lived in a big apartment hotel near Central Park. He ventured out only after dusk, and even then, when he passed an arc lamp, he hurried lest somebody recognize him and smile. Fox believed that all New York was laughing at him—a thought that caused endless cursing in new and fantastic profanity.

To be tricked by a big hick from Alaska, to be shown up and beaten by this boob in the presence of newspaper men! Good God, whoever heard of such a mess? Sometimes, in spite of the scars on his face, he could not make himself believe all that had happened to himself—to Douglas Fox!

What maddened him most was that he could think of no retaliation. His hands were tied. He could do nothing to square things with this giant dumb-bell from Kalvik Island—nothing at all except to wish him evil with all his heart and soul. He thought of and discarded plan after plan during his convalescence only to discover that the best he could do was to hate Jonathan Hayes. The utter futility of hating without a chance to demonstrate his hate made the man ill.

Fox's rage reached a climax the day he read in his morning paper that Hayes was going to take an expedition to Alaska to recover the fortune in sealskins about which all the world had heard. The paper informed him that the expedition had the backing of Irving Beach, well known hunter of big game, who meant to accompany Hayes.

Beach, of all men! Fox remembered how Beach had warned him against the game he had played. Beach believed all the time that the sealskins existed. Now he was going after them.

Fox clasped his head in his hands and groaned loud in his helplessness. Suppose Beach found the skins! Suppose Hayes were on the level—and that he, Fox, were the sucker—too smart to know a good thing when it came along? If that ever got into the newspapers!

He began to rage up and down his apartment, and his wife, who knew his rages to her sorrow, put on her furs and ordered a taxi. To spend the day shopping, leaving Douglas to work off his rage alone, was the part of discretion for Ada.

In the midst of his raging Fox was aware that the telephone kept ringing insistently. Finally he snatched up the instrument and roared an answer.

"Gentleman to see you on important business," said the operator.

"Can't see anybody." Fox slammed up the receiver.

Presently the tinkling began again and goaded him to another answer. "Mr. Fox?" a man's voice asked.

"Well?"

"I want to talk to you, Mr. Fox. Got a business proposition."

"Well?"

"If you don't mind I'll call and explain it—"

"Explain it now."

"It's about Hayes—and his sealskins—"

The unknown got no further. Fox bellowed something without words or sense and slammed up the telephone.

Soon after he was aware of a knocking at the door and answered it in a towering rage. No sooner was the door unlatched than, in spite of all he could do, it was pushed open and a man entered the apartment. He was a short, broad-shouldered, chunky man with an aggressive red-brown beard. He came through the door and shoved Fox aside as if such things were child's play.

"I told you I wanted to talk business to you," the stranger remarked with surprising gentleness. "Now, Mr. Fox, really you must give me a quarter of an hour of your time. Come, let's sit down!"

"Who the hell are you?" Fox demanded.

"My name is Cook. Captain of a schooner. I used to be quite a friend of your protégé, Jonathan Hayes. Perhaps he's mentioned my name?"

"Darius Cook!"

Cook smiled. "I see he has mentioned my name! Suppose we sit down and be comfortable?"

Fox collapsed in a chair and stared at Darius Cook. The promoter's face was beaded with sweat and the hand with which he wiped it shook unsteadily. He attempted an apology.

"You've got to excuse me, Cook. My nerves are all on edge this morning. And when you said sealskins—"

"You've been reading the morning papers," Cook guessed. "Well, I think I can interest you in this little expedition after sealskins. I really think I can!"

"Oh, you do!" Fox snorted with heavy sarcasm.

"Yes, I do. There's a fortune in it for the man who finds that bay Hayes knows about."

"I don't believe it."

"No, I judged by newspaper accounts you didn't." Cook smiled. Fox's face grew red, then purple. Cook tactfully ignored his state of mind. "I believe in those skins," he said briskly. "I believe in them enough so that I'm fitting out a little expedition of my own to get them—"

"You are!"

"I am, indeed—"

"How the devil can you? You don't know where they are—"

"But Hayes does. And I'm going to let Hayes lead the way—then beat him to it. Simple, isn't it?"

"So simple it sounds silly to me—"

"No, it doesn't, Fox! Don't pretend—"

"Who says I'm pretending? I tell you I don't believe for a minute in this hop-head vision of a fortune in sealskins. What d'you take to get that way—"

"Tut, tut!" Cook remonstrated gently. "You know you believe—now. Because you know Hayes is not a—er—a promoter. He has nothing in the world to gain from this except finding the pelts. Whatever were your opinions, Mr. Fox, you have changed them. And have you stopped to consider just how you are going to feel when the news leaks out that Hayes got the skins? How will you like it when you find the last laugh is on you? Have you thought of that?"

Fox groaned and clasped his head between his hands. "Oh, go to the devil!" he said wearily.

"But perhaps it's not too late. Why not join me and beat Hayes to it?" Cook suggested hopefully.

Fox uncovered his face and eyed his visitor with signs of hope.

Then Captain Darius Cook went on with the air of a man who has nothing to conceal. "I need some backing. If you want to buy a part interest I will welcome you. And, Fox, I also feel that you can be of help in carrying out this plan—a great deal of help. You're a brainy man. In my crude way I also am intelligent. And this is a job for brainy men. Now, does it occur to you that perhaps you and I need each other?"

"Captain Cook," Fox exclaimed with more interest than he had displayed for some weeks in anything but hating, "you've got me interested. Your selling talk is immense. Now let's hear the details. Have a cigar?"

CHAPTER XX

TROUBLES AND TELEGRAMS

AL SAPLEY STOOD before a long mirror in the little parlor of a suite of rooms in the New State Hotel in Seattle. He was costumed strangely and wonderfully—and was admiring the complete effect for the first time.

The bald-headed little crook had a brand new sombrero on his head—a sombrero with a high-peaked crown and a wide leather band studded with bright brass nailheads. The great hat seemed to weigh him down. His coat was a mackinaw of a pattern so eloquent it might be termed a riot. Red and green were its chief characteristics, red and green arranged in checkerboard pattern, with a complementary pattern of orange and black by way of relief. His lean, corded neck stuck out of a bright flannel shirt, and an orange tie bulged out above the top of a buckskin vest. His trousers were of new and very yellow corduroy, and were stuffed into knee-length leather hunting boots. He had not neglected a pistol and leather holster. Altogether he considered himself equipped to tackle any hardships or adventures a wilderness could offer.

Marion Reade entered quietly, observed the pantomime before the mirror and opened her eyes wide. "Wow! What are you, a dog and pony show?"

Al cackled. "This is my new outfit. I'm *au fait* now for anything in the line of gold camps, placer diggin's, blizzards, stampedes, nuggets, sealskins, polar bears or mosquitoes. First thing this morning I spotted a store where they sell the real thing to

164

loggers and trappers and such like, and I gave 'em orders to fit me out complete."

"I don't think they missed anything." Marion smiled. "You look like a regular six-reel cowboy thriller. I've been out buying some things myself, but I see now I haven't the imagination for this sort of thing. I've got to hand it to you!"

Al wrinkled his brow suspiciously. "Are you kidding me, Marion? On the level, don't this look all right? I told the bird in the store I was going up to Alaska, and he took a good look at me and handed me this. That store's been outfitting men since the big gold strike of '96. They ought to know. Where's Hayes? He can tell me—"

"Not back yet."

"Did he go out with Beach?"

"Yes, to look over the steamer and make sure everything is ready. Don't bother any more about the outfit, Al. It's got to do. We're going to try to get away some time tonight if that chartered boat is ready, as it should be—"

"Sail tonight?"

She nodded.

"Aw, hell, I ought to have a couple of days to break in these boots. They're hurting my dogs something awful!"

"Then you'll have to break them in aboard ship. I don't believe Hayes planned this outing for the health of your feet."

"I guess I'll hustle right out and give the town a treat before it's too late," Al said, brightening.

When he had gone Marion busied herself with lists and memoranda, but she kept wondering about Al Sapley.

A week before they left New York Sapley had come to Hayes. "Say, listen, sucker," Al said humbly, "if I did anything to make you sore I want to square myself. You did a great piece of work when you showed up Douglas Fox. He's had that coming to him for a long time—and I'm strong for you! Can't we be pals again?"

Hayes's forgiveness had been instant and complete. It developed then that Al was in need.

"When you clouted Fox you also kicked me out of a job," he explained. "Of course I'm glad you did it, and all that—it's a fine thing—but these sudden reforms sure raise hell with the innocent bystanders, and I'm bystander-in-chief at this ruction. It's a cold world when you're down, maybe you've noticed that—and I seem to be losing my pep. Ten years ago a thing like being out of a job just made me laugh. Now I can't even get a giggle out of it. Wonder if I'm getting old!"

Hayes, busy as he was, had time to worry about Al. It was he who proposed bringing Sapley on the expedition. "He's useful in lots of ways," he argued. "He's shrewder than any of us about anything that's crooked—and he might come in handy if we did run up against Cook."

Hayes had his way about it, and Sapley was given work. Marion reminded him, "The last time I saw you, you were going to shoot Hayes on sight. What's changed your mind?"

"Say, don't rub it in, Marion! I was wrong, and I admit it. Hayes is one big, fine, square guy, and I'm for him! Ain't that reason enough?"

Marion wondered privately if it were reason enough. The reason did not quite accord with her notion of the man. But Sapley showed a great willingness to do anything he was told. He was used for various errands and performed faithfully. He was a favorite with Hayes, and even Beach admitted it might be well to have one more man on whom they could depend in case of an emergency.

Beach and Hayes came into the room hurriedly. They were wrapped in raincoats, dripping wet, and flushed from the cold air and with excitement. She saw at first glance that something had gone wrong.

"It's the charter," Beach exclaimed, answering her look. "That steamer that was to be waiting—ready for us—isn't."

"It isn't ready?"

"It isn't here! It sailed three days ago for Grays Harbor to load lumber for San Pedro—"

"Why, how could it?"

"That's the queer part of it," Hayes said gloomily. "It's more than I can understand."

Beach explained, "I wired a ship broker here, you know? They wired back that I could get this boat—just what we needed. I wired orders to charter her and money was forwarded. Everything was all right. Then, the morning after we left New York, the broker got a telegram releasing the boat—breaking off our charter—and forfeiting our deposit. Can you beat it? *That wire was signed with my name!*"

"The boat is gone?"

"Gone. Chartered next day to a local shipper and loading lumber right now, I suppose."

"Gone," Hayes echoed glumly, "and as far as we can find out there is not another thing anywhere near her size. Nothing lying idle on Puget Sound that we can use!"

They looked at each other long and silently.

"It doesn't seem to make sense!" Marion exclaimed finally. "That telegram—signed with your name, Beach—"

"A forgery, of course. Anybody might have sent it. I'm having the telegraph people do what they can to trace it. But what gets me is that the sender knew just where to direct his messages— to our shipping agent and the bank. And who in the world would have a reason to go to all that trouble?"

"Cook! That's my guess," said Hayes.

"Yes, and my guess. Obviously it was done to delay us—and if Cook still has an idea of getting those skins, perhaps by following our lead, he might want to delay us. But the big question is, how did Cook find out?"

"Every move has been a secret among the three of us," Hayes added.

They looked at each other again, long and hopelessly.

"What's this, a Quaker meeting?" Al Sapley had come into the room and surveyed them with astonishment.

Even Al's extraordinary attire passed unnoticed for the time. Ignoring him, Beach said earnestly, "If it is Cook the big thing for us to do is get moving fast. We must have another boat, and right away."

"I should think there would be lots of boats around with all this water," Marion contributed.

"Not the kind we need. But we'll find one—a steamer, if possible. Hayes, I'm going back to the Merchants' Exchange again and perhaps wire to San Francisco."

"I'll make inquiries along the waterfront if you think that will help," Hayes volunteered.

Al chimed in, "Say, ain't there something I could do?"

Hayes, who had been studying him with growing wonder, shook his head. "Better go back to the fancy dress ball," he advised.

At lunch, when they all gathered again, Hayes had a suggestion. "I heard of a schooner we might use," he said. "She's one of the Gloucester type halibut fishers, built like a yacht and able to sail as fast as a lot of steamships. Besides, she has a gas engine for auxiliary power. The cargo space is all we need, and there's a chance to get her, I think. The price for halibut is low, and she's laid off. I have the name and address of the principal owner, if you think he's worth talking to."

Beach agreed at once. "She might do very well. And the principal thing is to find our boat as soon as we can. This telegram business—our broken charter—that doesn't strike me as very reassuring some way—"

"Did the telegraph people trace the fraud message?" Hayes asked.

"As far as they could! It was sent from the Pennsylvania Station the morning after we left New York. You can imagine what chance there is to find the sender!"

The address Hayes had was in Ballard, a suburb. Beach decided they must have an automobile.

"Shall I go?" Marion asked.

"No. Better stay here. The Merchants' Exchange is making some inquiries for me. There might be a message, and you can help by keeping track of things."

"Well," Al volunteered brightly, "I don't suppose I could help you much about a ship. I never rented one, except one of those boats on the Central Park lake one time. But I can do *my* bit! I'll just chase out and find a rent car for you."

Hayes watched that queer, boylike figure with its wizen neck and face, flapping its grotesque finery as it hurried down the long dining room. He smiled. "He's always anxious to help! You can't help liking that fellow."

The gray, rainy afternoon wore into darkness, and Marion waited impatiently for the return of Beach and Hayes. Al was in and out of their suite half a dozen times, in high spirits and very busy. "Forgot to lay in some blankets," he explained. "And while I'm about it, maybe I'd better get me a coffee pot and frying pan. What do you think?"

"I would," Marion smiled scornfully. "And if I were you I'd try to buy a patent gold rocker and a collapsible rowboat somewhere. Too bad you haven't a Sears-Roebuck catalogue, it would suggest so many little helpful things!"

"Kid me all you want!" Al cackled, "I ain't going to take any chances on sleeping cold out on some glacier. You never can tell on a trip like this. No, sir! You never can tell!"

The two men came back finally, long past dinner hour. They tramped into the room dripping rain water. They looked weary and very sober.

"Too late," Beach said, answering Marion's look. "Our car broke down. It took that thick-headed chauffeur an hour and a half to fix it—and all the time all it needed was a slight adjustment of the manifold intake!"

"You didn't find your man?"

"We found him," Hayes groaned. "And found that somebody else had chartered his boat—this afternoon! While we were wallowing in the mud around that automobile!"

"Great cat!" cried Al. "There's a hoodoo riding with us!"

"There is," Beach said grimly. "And if this kind of luck repeats itself again I'll begin to think it's more than a hoodoo—" Hayes agreed soberly. "It begins to look queer. It looks like something more than just bad luck!"

But Marion smiled brightly. "Don't let it get on your nerves! It won't repeat! At least, I think not. I have found a steamer!" She handed them a small Kodak print with smiling triumph. "Would that answer what we need?" she asked.

Hayes and Beach examined the picture of a small, wooden cargo boat and nodded. "Looks like it! Where? What—"

"A man called this afternoon. He said the Merchants' Exchange gave him Beach's name. He's an old skipper, a tough, battered, tobacco-chewing old downeaster. His name is Blye, and he claims he has the owner's authority to make a charter for this boat. The name of it is the *Karluk* and it's here in this harbor. He says he can get his crew together, load coal and supplies, and be ready to steam from here by tomorrow night."

"Splendid!" Hayes exclaimed.

"Where is the man?" Beach demanded. "How can we reach him?"

"Waiting at this moment downstairs in the lobby. I made him wait."

They sent at once for Captain Blye. He proved to be squat and round, running to paunch, but for all that a toughened, alert and capable person of uncertain age. His big nose and protuberant chin suggested a caricature of the first Napoleon. His eye was a frosty blue and he talked with a pronounced Yankee twang, very economical of words.

They were so favorably impressed with Blye that directly they had dined they accompanied him to the waterfront and took a launch out to the *Karluk*. She proved to be about what they needed, a small cargo steamer, stoutly built, with sufficient accommodations for their party.

They sat in a chill, damp and rather stuffy little cabin about a table lighted by an overhead oil lamp while Beach and Blye finished negotiations.

"The exact destination of this voyage is our own business," Beach explained.

"Agreeable," twanged Blye.

"The shipping articles can make it Dutch Harbor and other ports of Western Alaska. That will cover it, I think—"

"Right."

"You can find your crew?"

"Got 'em, mostly."

"And get all supplies and coal tomorrow—"

"Yep."

"And we sail?"

"Ten thirty. Tomorrow night. From the bunkers, foot of Main Street."

"You hear?" Beach addressed them all. "Everybody must have his stuff aboard and be ready. And, another thing, Captain Blye, all of you, don't talk—"

"Never talk," said Blye.

"Don't anybody talk. The less said about our plans the better. This—this hoodoo—if it is a hoodoo—is not to get any encouragement by knowing what we are about to do."

"Cat's got my tongue," Al Sapley crackled.

"See that it keeps it," Hayes advised shortly.

The following busy day it seemed that the bad luck had deserted them for all time. Supplies from the ship chandlers were pouring aboard the *Karluk*. Blye had a crew rounded up and signed before the commissioner by early afternoon and the steamer shifted to the bunkers where tons of coal went thundering into her hold. Hayes, Marion, and Beach completed a few necessary errands ashore and their luggage came aboard promptly.

Al Sapley was last to arrive. He came in a taxi that was making heavy weather of it under a deckload of stuff such as few arctic explorers could better. Al had rolls and bundles and canvas bags. Outside these snowshoes were strapped and cooking utensils.

Hayes met him on deck. "What's all this stuff?" he demanded.

"Mine. That's my outfit. The rest of it's coming aboard in a minute."

Hayes frowned. "No, it isn't. Wait! Let me look at it!" He bent over the bundles, unlashing them rapidly. One by one he picked up and threw to one side frying pan, coffee pot, a collapsible camp stove, a canvas water bucket, a roll of blankets, snowshoes, fur mittens—all manner of sporting goods store supplies.

"Hey!" Al piped aggrievedly. "What you trying to do?"

"Outfitting you right. Now, take all that junk ashore. You may keep the rifle—"

"Don't I get nothing else?"

"Not a thing. If I had time I'd make you buy some decent clothes. You'll scare the natives into hysteria! Now, hustle!"

Al turned on the grinning taxi driver. "Shut up!"

"I didn't say anything—"

"You looked it! Get that stuff off'n here. You hear? Show some speed!"

"You've got just five minutes to make it in," Hayes advised Al. "See that you don't miss the boat." Sapley staggered down the plank under a load of duffel; he went meekly enough, but his lips were twisting over whispered opinions of them all, and threats. Yet he was grinning, too—grinning as if all this were a joke.

Lines were cast off and men's voices shouted orders to the

dark wharf below. A signal clanged in the engine room of the *Karluk* and the vessel began to vibrate to the churn of the screw.

Hayes, Beach, and Marion, wrapped against the drizzle, stood on the bridge where Blye paced, a shapeless, round bundle, supported on two stubby legs set wide apart. The *Karluk* cleared her dock and pushed into Seattle Harbor. The lights of the city of many hills rose at their right.

Marion grasped Hayes's arm. "We're going!" she whispered. "Old Timer, we're on our way at last! And we're going to put it over, Hayes; I feel it in my bones. Say you're glad!"

Hayes breathed deep. "I'm more than that! I'm thankful. And a whole lifetime won't be enough to pay you back for this wonderful thing you did. You have saved me!"

"I wonder what in the world's keeping Sapley," Beach broke in. "I saw him come aboard. Funny he's not around. He always is when he's not needed!"

But Al Sapley was not aboard. He had slipped ashore one last time, and when the *Karluk* cleared her dock he emerged from the black shadows of the coal pockets and watched her sail. As he watched Sapley broke into his high, cackling laughter and his mirth doubled him up and held him helpless for a time.

Finally he recovered breath for speech. "Oof!" he gasped. "Wow! Sail—go ahead and sail, you suckers! You boobs! You dumb-bells! That's right, sail! But when you find out what I know—*whoopee!*"

He stood in the dark there, an absurd figure, but venomous in his unhealthy glee, thumbing his nose after the departing steamer *Karluk*.

CHAPTER XXI

WHISPERS IN THE DARK

UNHAPPY WEATHER HUNG on the heels of the *Karluk* as though the night of drizzle in which she left Seattle Harbor was some sort of magic spell that could not be banished. It was still too early in the year to hope for much relief, and the North Pacific was turbulent with gales and squalls of snow and sleet, damp, clinging fogs and temperatures that made men shiver in spite of heavy mackinaws and pea-jackets.

From the time the stout wooden steamer dropped Cape Flattery Light they would be out of sight of land until they raised Kodiak Island. Captain Blye had orders to find this landfall. Then Hayes would give him further instructions.

Blye displayed no surprise at his peculiar orders. He nodded assent and went about his business. They saw the captain only at meals, and not always then. Socially he could scarcely be called an addition to any circle. With his peculiar economy of words he could manage to answer the most involved question or discussion in five seconds flat, and he never argued the point. If undisturbed, he ate without a word, and sometimes his frosty blue eyes stole sly glances about the table. But what he thought of them all and their enterprise he kept to himself.

When they established beyond a doubt that Al Sapley was left on the dock in Seattle, Hayes suggested stopping at Fort Townsend to send a telegram. The matter was discussed and vetoed.

"He meant to stay ashore," Beach argued. "There isn't any other explanation. He's a rotten little quitter!"

"Unless he got tangled up in all that junk and fell off the dock," Marion suggested.

Hayes could not understand it. "But he meant to go! He was so enthusiastic! He did nothing that last day but buy things—like a small boy going camping."

"Then the small boy got cold feet when you cut him down to one rifle with which to face the wilderness," Beach grinned.

Marion suggested another explanation. "Al Sapley has a twisted sense of humor. He's a great little practical joker. I've seen him go to no end of trouble to make a fool of himself and then get his reward by laughing at the people who were simple enough to think he did not know better. It's a queer, inverted sort of egotism. It would be like the little rat, exactly, to go to all that trouble and mean to fool us all the time! He's probably laughing to himself right now."

Hayes exclaimed hopelessly, "I can't make it out. He seemed so anxious to go and help us!" He was bewildered and hurt by Sapley's desertion. He liked Sapley.

The routine of the *Karluk* was monotonous to the point of madness. Bad weather kept them closely indoors. They had only their thoughts for company. But as the steamer neared her western Alaskan destination a restlessness came over Jonathan Hayes. It was as if the man smelled the land that was his home. He was much on deck in spite of sleet and damp, staring into the vast, gray, ever-shifting horizon where the snow ghosts danced. With each breath he seemed to expand and grow. All trace of the weariness, the beaten look he had worn on Broadway was gone. He laughed often and sang old songs under his breath.

Marion, muffled against the damp and cold, ventured out after the evening meal, determined to get some exercise and fresh air in spite of weather. She discovered Hayes by the rail near the bow, his usual post. He was staring steadily into the blackness and she heard him singing to himself. The *Karluk* pitched and sent her staggering against him.

Hayes caught her and held her fast. "You have no business going out alone on deck," he growled. "Especially at night. Suppose you had gone over the rail—who would have seen you in this muck?"

"Don't be sore when you ought to feel so happy, Hayes!"

"I am happy. I never felt like this in all my life, so alive and full of hope and dead sure that I'm going to whittle out life to suit myself!" Hayes established her firmly against the rail and he shielded her there, safe. "And how about you?" he asked.

"Me!"

"Yes. How do you feel? What do you think about all day, I wonder? I wonder if you're getting the solid satisfaction—happiness—you ought to get from doing a big thing? Because you did a big thing, the biggest thing any human being can do. You picked up a man who was beaten by life and set him on his feet again. Doesn't that make you feel proud?"

"Oh, that! Hayes, you will insist on making a mountain out of little things. All I did was give you some advice about where to get money—and a few things like that. You did the dirty work yourself. And heaven knows I owed you what little help I could give! Set you on your feet? I didn't have half as much to do with that as I did about rolling you in the mud in the first place!" She shivered.

Hayes said softly, "You're a very splendid—courageous—wonderful woman, Marion—"

"Oh, please, not that—"

"Just that! My dear, my dear, if you knew how I have watched you these last few weeks, how I've appreciated the things you did so bravely and cheerfully—and laughed at and called nothing! And how I wished I had the words to say to you that I understood and loved you for them. And once I called you a tinsel woman! You remember? Over there on Kalvik, somewhere out there ahead of us, when we stood on the beach and saw the yacht coming? Marion! Can you ever forgive me that?" Marion heard this in a kind of shivering delight—a delight that was a good part terror. Hayes must not be let to say these things! Her bargain with Beach was made and she never welshed on her promises, as Beach reminded her when she made it. Hayes must not be let to hope—not even for a minute. She summoned all her will. "Hayes," she said sharply in her best Broadway manner, "let's not get sloppy! The weather's bad enough—"

"I'm talking sense. I'm talking the truest common sense there is, dear, when I say I love and reverence you—"

Marion giggled audaciously. "You look as if you were preaching my funeral eulogy!" She mimicked his words, " 'I love and reverence you!' Oh, Hayes, when you roll your eyes that way!"

Her words hurt him. She saw it in his face and the glowing eyes and in his manner. He was hurt, and the knowledge hurt her until she wanted to cry out.

After a silence Hayes said quietly, "I am very sorry if I seem ridiculous. What I feel is not amusing—"

She caught his arm tight and pressed it. "I know! I do understand. But—" Hayes's arms were about her. He held her tightly while he said hurriedly, "Then you know that I love you. That I have loved you from the minute you came to Kalvik—always—in spite of everything! And now—now that I'm going to succeed, going to prove myself against that world of yours, I want you to keep your promise and listen to me—"

"Promise!"

Fright had made her voice harsh.

"Yes, your promise, made to me that night on Fox's yacht. You promised then you would wait for me—until I succeeded—"

"Yes, *until you succeeded!*" She managed to laugh again, mocking him. "Careful, sucker! You're not out of the woods yet. This is no time to yell!"

"I will do what I set out to do!"

"So you say—"

"I'm not boasting without cause. I'm going to do this thing. And then you must listen when I ask you to marry me!"

"I—if I made that promise, Hayes—"

"You did make that promise!"

"Yes, yes! But not now! You must not ask me now! You must not—"

"You don't care! It's no use asking you?"

She pulled away from him, panting a little. She was terrified at what she might say, realizing that her secret must be kept from him still—kept from him until he had done what he set out to do—and terrified lest he guess that secret.

"You—you don't know me. Not really," she said hurriedly. "How can you know what goes on inside my head—in my heart? If you could see what is there, how utterly trivial I am—how worthless—"

"Marion!"

"I am! I'm exactly what you said—a tinsel woman. It's Broadway—it's in my blood. Hayes, can't you understand I'm not your sort—I'm not worth it!"

"You sha'n't say that! That's not true!"

"It is true! It's true. True! Hayes, you must understand. I—*I'm not even decent.*"

"What's this?"

"In my thoughts I'm not. In my heart I'm not. I'm no good. No good! A rotten, bad lot. Not decent!"

Hayes was protesting hotly. "Marion, this is all nonsense. You must never say a thing like that! I won't let you say it—"

But she interrupted so earnestly he was silenced. "Take me to my stateroom. Now. Don't say a word more. Not one word. And don't let me talk of this again. Do you understand? Not now!"

Hayes took her arm and led her to her little cabin. At the door he said gravely, "Nothing you say can frighten me—or change me. I love you."

The door was slammed in his face. On the inside Marion leaned weakly against the panels. "Oh, dear God!" she sobbed.

Hayes tramped the deck a couple of hours more, soaked without and raging hot within. Finally he went to the little general cabin that was dining room and saloon and office at times, and found Beach yawning over a novel.

"You look like a drowned rat," Beach said. "What's the matter with you?"

"Nothing."

"It looks like nothing! Your face is whiter than this page. Here, take a drink!"

Hayes drank what was given him without any consciousness of the act.

Beach made him lay off his wet coat. "I'll deal you a few poker hands," he suggested cheerfully.

"Cards! I haven't the stomach for that tonight, Beach."

"Too bad you don't like cards. Stupid things! But they keep a man from eating his heart out with this damned waiting— waiting!"

"Waiting is pretty nearly over," Hayes said. "Two days, three at the outside, and we ought to reach that "—he looked about sharply—"we ought to reach our port," he amended.

"Suppose Blye's reckoning is all right?" Beach grunted. "No landfall since we left Flattery! Not even a clear day to shoot the sun! All he's got to go by is the log. If this boat's as fast as he claims I'm a poor guesser!"

"The thick weather is one blessing, at least—"

"What's that, Hayes?"

"Cook—if Cook happens to be following us. He would have a sweet time keeping on our trail these days!"

Beach looked thoughtful, a little encouraged. "I suppose he would! And it did look in Seattle as if somebody was on our trail. I'm glad it's going to be decided soon! I can remember pleasanter excursions than this—"

"It's pretty fine of you to come, Beach. You know how much this means to me. I—I hope you know how much I appreciate your help—all your trouble—your friendship—" Hayes choked. "I can't say it—tonight. But, thanks!" He grasped Beach's hand and turned away. "I'm going to bed."

Beach looked long and thoughtfully at the door after it had closed on Hayes. "He doesn't know!" he thought. "He hasn't even a suspicion yet! I'm almost sorry for that big innocent—but we can't both have Marion—and I mean to!"

Marion found her little cabin intolerable. She could not sleep, she could not rest or even stay still because of the jangle of emotions Hayes had started. She wrapped herself finally and went out into the night again. A high wind and the pitching of the *Karluk* made walking the deck almost impossible. She found a shelter in the angle of the deck house near the bridge and sat down on the coaming of a skylight. The vessel's stack was close by and radiated warmth. The fresh air was delicious. Her aching head quieted.

Her mind could not leave her troubles. It was a ghastly mess and no mistake. Yet a month ago this would have seemed the logical solution. A couple of months ago to promise Beach would have been the realization of an ambition. She was doing what she had planned to do last summer: winning the man so many ambitious girls had tried for—and doing Hayes a good turn besides. Why wasn't she glad about it? Why wasn't she tickled pink? Life had got itself so balled up she couldn't be sure about anything—yes, one thing! When Hayes found out her promise to Beach—that would be tough on Hayes—pretty darn tough!

Yet the warmth and the stinging freshness of the salt air brought quiet of a sort. She ceased to think at all, lulled by the unceasing harping of the wind in the stays that held the big stack, and the regular roar and long-drawn hiss of waves racing past in the blackness. Perhaps she even dozed a little.

The murmur of two men's voices caught her wandering attention. She realized sleepily that she was leaning against the wall of the deck house and beneath a cabin port. Somebody was talking in there—two men talking—questions and answers and a chuckle or two. One of them must be Captain Blye. The other—

Marion stiffened bolt upright. She did not breathe in the intensity of her effort to listen. An ice-cold wave of fright went tingling through her, a true nightmare fright, for her reason tried to reassure her she had not heard right.

She craned her head and glanced up at the cabin port. It had been screwed open a crack for ventilation. She rose to her feet to press her ear closer, though the effort to coordinate her fear-bound muscles was agonizing. She clung to the wall, raising her head slowly, fearfully toward the port.

A murmured phrase leaked out, then Blye's nasal twang. "Wait. Port's open. Colder than Greenland tonight."

A few inches from her head the captain's hand clamped the window into its socket.

Presently she ventured to look, hoping that a glance into the cabin would dispel her nightmare phantasy. But a curtain had been drawn across the glass.

Marion ran down the deck, staggering with the lurching of the plunging steamer, careless of all risk of falling, of being washed off by some marauding wave.

Beach and Hayes had cabins side by side, next to her own. All opened on deck and were in the after-deck house. She hammered frantically at one door, then the other, whispering the men's names.

Beach, who had scarcely entered his cabin, opened his door first. She clutched at him when Hayes's door opened and he came out, coatless.

Marion dragged them both into Beach's cabin. She was white and breathless, and her brown eyes were big and round. She looked like a child terrified by a bad dream.

"On this boat!" she whispered, shuddering and clawing at them. "On this very boat. He's on this boat!"

"Who? What? Marion, child, you're shivering! You're sick!"

They pushed her gently onto Beach's berth, and Beach made her drink something warming from his flask.

"Easy now!" Hayes was saying comfortingly. "What's scared you? Who's on this boat?"

"Whoever it is won't hurt you. We'll look after it," Beach reassured her. "Now, who—"

"Cook!"

The men stared blankly.

"Captain Darius Cook!" Marion repeated frantically. "He is! I heard him—heard him talking. In the cabin. With Blye. I was at the window. I heard Cook's voice."

Hayes slammed out of the cabin and reappeared in a moment, fully dressed. His hand slipped a pistol into the coat pocket as he came in. He found Beach ready.

"Stay right here," they advised the girl.

"Don't—don't do—anything—"

"Nothing foolish," Hayes promised, and they hurried to the deck.

CHAPTER XXII

A PLACE WITHOUT A NAME

BEACH GRASPED HAYES'S arm and halted him.

"Wait," he murmured. "We've got to use a little strategy. If that should be Cook we want to know it, but we do not want to let him know we know—not until we've thought things out. Let's figure out how to go at this—"

"You're right, Beach! If Cook is aboard we could get rid of him at Kodiak if we surprised him—"

"I can't believe it's he! Marion's been dreaming!"

"You don't know Cook. I do! Now, what's your plan?"

"I'll talk to Blye. If our man's hid in that cabin you'll have a chance to look about. See what you can find out—but don't give yourself away!" Beach laughed shortly. "What utter rot! You'd think this was a melodrama. Marion must have dreamed the girl's unstrung!"

Even Hayes smiled a moment. "I begin to agree with you. Well, we had better look. It will satisfy her."

Beach's knock at the cabin door brought a sharp query from Captain Blye. "Well?"

"It's Beach and Hayes. May we come in?"

After a moment of waiting Blye opened the door. The captain was coatless and without shoes. He rubbed his eyes as they entered.

The master's cabin was a little larger than the staterooms, but equally bleak. There were two seats and a small business desk built into the bulkhead. Against the inner wall of the room,

in an alcove, was his berth, the curtains drawn. Their first searching glances discovered everything as it should be, except those
drawn curtains of the berth—and that was no unusual thing.

Blye maintained his customary silence as they seated themselves. He was the picture of a man roused from a nap and not
overwhelmed with delight at the interruption.

"We got to wondering about progress," Beach was explain-
ing affably as he leaned near the captain. "Hope you don't mind
the interruption too much. You see neither of us knows anything
of navigation—"

"Thought you owned a yacht?"

"Well! You must have been looking up my family tree!"

"Naturally. Business. Might say common sense—"

"I do own a yacht. But I don't know how to run it. Well, are
you going to deliver the goods—will we see Kodiak tomorrow?"

Blye reached into the business desk and produced his log.
He picked up paper and pencil and began to explain his calculations to Beach.

The sportsman leaned forward, all attention and questions,
managing by his bulk to shield Hayes from the captain. Hayes
rose as if to come closer and look over their shoulders. The ship
lurched and he staggered with it, straight back against the closed
curtains of the berth.

The curtains parted with his weight and he half sat, half
sprawled on the floor.

The maneuver had all the appearance of a landsman's clum-
siness at sea.

Blye raised a frosty blue eye.

"Seasick?" he twanged sharply.

Hayes looked apologetic. "I never could make my feet track
on a boat!" He rose and rejoined them, bracing his swaying
figure against the wall.

Beach studied the captain's calculations with wrinkled brow.
"It beats me!" he exclaimed. "You mean to say without anything

to go by but this dead reckoning, you expect to pick up a pin point on the globe? God!"

"Ain't be'n off yet. Be'n sailin' sixty-five years. Never off more'n fifty miles."

Both men murmured appropriate applause. "When you pick up the island," Hayes said with a yawn, "go round into Shelikof Strait. We'll have to stop near Uyak for a bit."

"Stop!" Blye exclaimed sharply.

Beach looked a little surprised.

"Native pilot in the village there," Hayes murmured. "We're going to need his help to get to where we're going."

Blye shrugged. "Look here. Hope you understand this ain't no *bidarka*. This boat draws water and I ain't goin' to throw her away on no reef."

"That's why I want my pilot, captain."

Beach yawned and proposed they go to bed. Blye saw them out with his usual emphatic silence.

Safely away from the cabin Beach asked sharply: "Well?"

"That cabin is as empty as the day it was built. Nobody is hiding in it. No sign of anybody having been there."

"I thought as much! Marion dreamed it!"

"Looks that way. But it's a queer dream. Beach, I don't like that kind of dream. We'll look sharp and ask some questions of the crew tomorrow. I threw in the stop at Uyak just to make sure we had an excuse for delay—if we should need one."

Tactful inquiries and detective work convinced Beach and Hayes that Marion had suffered from nightmare. Life aboard the *Karluk* did not deviate at all from the dull routine of any small freighter. In the morning light Marion herself was in-clined to doubt events of the night before.

"I suppose I'll be seeing pink elephants and goldfish wearing high silk hats, next!" She smiled wanly. "The coffee they make on this boat is bad enough, but I never dreamed it would do that to me!"

Late in the day with better weather they made out the distant bulk of Kodiak Island. Captain Blye was right. He accepted their congratulations with a bark. "Ain't no damn fool!"

During the following day they rounded Kodiak at a respectful distance and came to anchor finally off a barren shore. "The village lies in that cove," Hayes exclaimed. "Set me ashore in a boat."

Blye was fussy.

"Don't need no pilot."

"I think we do." Hayes insisted. "He knows the place well— and it's not a healthy place if you don't know it."

"Don't trust any Eskimos!"

"They're not Eskimos. Aleuts, Indians. I know this man, captain, and I advise you he may be very useful."

"I'll go with you, then. Ain't goin' to take no pilot unless I see him. Responsible for this ship."

Hayes acquiesced readily.

Beach drew the Alaskan aside. "You really want this Indian?"

"Paul Oo-kat-lek is a good man. A friend of mine. We can use him. I hope he has some friends to bring along!"

But at the Aleut village disappointment waited. A few women were left in the skin houses. The men were hunting and might be gone for weeks. Blye listened suspiciously while Hayes talked with the squaws in the clicking, spitting, guttural tongue.

"What she say?" he inquired incessantly. When Hayes told him finally that the needed man was not available the captain grunted. "Glad of it. Damn Indians! Fish eaters!"

They were rowed aboard the *Karluk*. "Now where?" Captain Blye wanted to know.

"I'll show you," Hayes agreed. "Come up to the chart house."

For two days the *Karluk* steamed through lonely waters, on her port bow the bleak Alaskan coast, its mountain peaks a solid blue silhouette except where snow patches clung in ragged pattern. The weather relented and the sun favored them with a watery pallid light, but little warmth. It still circled below the zenith, and days still were short. Calmer waters became a slaty, cold blue. Nothing moved on their wide expanse. No sign of life could be seen on the coast. The world they were in had beauty, the majesty of great vistas and rugged picturesqueness, but no human touch, no human warmth. Marion, most susceptible to it, shivered often as she watched from the deck. They were so alone here, so utterly lost in this raw wilderness!

Hayes looked on the land with eyes alight. It was home again, for him. Beach was grave, but with a certain alertness, a sense of relief that their business soon would be done. But every hour increased Marion's dread. If only the ship were wrecked, if some accident only could turn them back! Of all things she dreaded most their shadowy destination, the bay of the glacier where Hayes's fortune lay. She knew that there would be written a chapter of her life she never could erase—a chapter of tragedy. There, Hayes must be told!

"Pretty nearly there!"

Beach had stopped beside her. He was smiling. "There's a thrill in this, isn't there? I used to dream about treasurehunting when I was a youngster. Laughed at it when I grew older. But you can't deny there's a real kick in it!"

"We are—almost there—really?"

"Look, we're cutting in toward shore now!"

The *Karluk's* course had changed. She was approaching the coast. A peak, higher than its neighbors, and crowned with a majestic diadem of white, rose directly ahead of the bows.

Beach pointed. "Under that mountain is a long inlet—a *fjord*. In there lies this glacier. Hayes says. In just a few hours we'll see it. We'll know. Today we may even see those pelts!"

Marion looked, but the landscape wavered before her eyes. "I—somehow, I can't believe it!"

"I know, I know!" Her hand was on the rail and Beach's covered it. He was smiling gently and pressed close beside her.

"It's the end of a long trail, isn't it, my dear? A hard trail. But you did a splendid thing for Hayes—"

"I did!" Her voice cracked. She drew away from him, facing him with eyes that were black and hard. "I did a splendid thing—for—Hayes! Beach—you are—quaint!" She laughed unsteadily.

"Why not? You put the chap on his feet. You've made it possible for him to hold up his head again. What's the matter?"

She shrugged with better self-control. "Nothing. Nothing's the matter."

He caught her sleeve and pulled her closer, gently. "It's been a pretty tough trail for me, too. Do you realize that? Do you, Marion?"

"I—yes, I suppose it has—"

"But I've tried to carry on—"

"You have carried on! You've done wonders!"

"Because of you, then. Because I had something waiting for me at the end of the trail. I've kept my share of the bargain, Marion."

"Yes."

"Well, thank Heaven, you're no welsher. You won't go back on your promise."

"No. I keep my promises."

"But you want to keep that promise? Say you do! You care for me, don't you? Marion, just one small payment in advance!" He bent near to kiss her.

She drew away, struggling. "Not here. Not now. Please, Beach! Later—I'll pay up!"

Beach laughed. "It's all right. I can wait. Look what I have to wait for!" He walked away smiling, humming cheerfully a silly little song from a new musical show.

Marion watched him go, experiencing odd emotions. This was the same Beach she had known for several years—yet a stranger. A total stranger! She realized with astonishment that she was afraid of Beach—afraid of this man she had bargained to marry! Beach was a stranger, unknown, a cause of mistrust and terror!

There was a stir of interest throughout the *Karluk*. News that the voyage was nearing its objective seemed to radiate by intuition. Several unkempt heads were thrust from ports below. A couple of coal-grimed men appeared in light of day and stared at the land and pointed. On the bridge Hayes and Beach and Blye stood together watching the coast. Their progress was slowed to a more cautious speed.

The feeling was infectious. Marion forgot everything else to share this excitement of discovery.

With the steamer's approach new hills and headlands seemed to swim toward them—to materialize and take new importance. The snow-capped peak overtopped everything, spread across the sky and rose toward the zenith until closer ridges eclipsed it.

The *Karluk* passed into a channel that began to narrow, a channel bordered by steep hills forested with black-green spruce and pine and fir, so steep that they rose from the water's edge in cliffs and ledges. Captain Blye had a small boat out, sounding the channel, and the *Karluk* drifted and crawled at a pace irritatingly slow.

The channel turned sharply. When they were around the bend Marion saw that it ended about a mile beyond this turn. At the end ramparts of ice gleamed in the late sunlight. It was the glacier, that immense, slow-moving river of ice that flowed forever from its source in the peak towering above to the sea. Where the ice met the water it made palisades and cliffs, colored with cold blues and greens, sometimes striking prismatic notes of fire from the glancing sun rays. As Marion looked there came from these cliffs a report like heavy artillery, and presently the widening circles of a great wave breaking the reflections of the still channel into fragments like some gigantic jig-saw picture puzzle.

"The glacier is sloughing," said Hayes's voice close by her. "It keeps that up day and night—forever and ever. Sounds like a battlefield. I've seen a piece as big as some of those New York skyscrapers split off—and the racket of it!"

Hayes loomed bigger, more alive than she had ever seen him. Excitement had tightened his mouth to a severe line and brought queer lights to his eyes. In spite of his casual manner the man evidently was feeling intensely.

"Beach and I are going to be rowed in," he went on. "You'll come?"

"If I'm wanted—"

"Wanted!" Beach exclaimed, joining them. "Do you mean to say you could resist the curiosity to see if our fortune's still there—after coming all this way!"

Two men were assigned to one of the *Karluk's* boats, and they were rowed toward the glacier, while Captain Blye groped his way to an anchorage as close in as he dared bring the steamer. Their boat was no more than a frail egg shell, its passengers pigmies, as they neared the towering ice walls that closed the channel. They were silent with awe at the fantastic towers, minarets and palisades of pure ice, the vast caverns and cracks that traversed it.

Hayes, at the tiller, veered the boat sharply as they came nearer. "It's not healthy. Too close," he exclaimed. "No fun having several thousand tons of that stuff drop on us."

Even as he spoke they exclaimed at the spectacle of a vast, jagged block tipping and tottering and cleaving with that terrifying, explosive crash of big guns. A wave generated by the ice fall came rolling toward them and Hayes turned the craft toward it, ordering the oarsmen to steady her until it had lifted them and passed, leaving them tossing in the choppy cross seas. Blocks of ice, ranging from splinters to bergs, bowed and rocked sedately all about them.

They passed along the front of the glacier to the right side of the *fjord* as one faced the mountain. Hayes steered their boat into a small cove and they landed. The two men were left to wait. Marion, Beach and Hayes went inland, the Alaskan leading.

"The cave is just over this shoulder," Hayes explained. "There's a little spur of the glacier left in here, dead ice, a sort of eddy or backwater out of the stream. The cave itself is rock, blocked with this ice—you'll see."

Hayes's voice shook a little. Beach was panting, and Marion's hand, pressed to her throat, gave silent notice of her distress. All of them were at a half trot and quite unaware of it.

They crossed the shoulder of rock, broke through low thickets of vine and bush and young alder, and Hayes, who plunged on ahead, was heard to shout: "All right! Marion—oh, Marion! We win!"

Marion ran and leaped down the slope, the pebbles rolling beneath her feet. Beach had shouted something and crashed on. When she came up the men were standing before a low, dark passage, the hole of the cave, peering, exclaiming, shaken with excitement.

But Marion's interest was not for the cave nor for the piled bundles of seal pelts stowed in its dusk, though Beach and Hayes were pointing and shouting to her to see. Her first glance and all her glances were at the face of Jonathan Hayes. The victory was his, and the pride and delight that glowed in his plain, usually sober face, the triumph sparkling in his dark eyes, all of it reflected its warm glow upon her.

Just for that look on Hayes's face, just for the man's pride in achievement she had planned and worked, risked and traded, and endured with patience these last few weeks. She thought at that moment that all she had done was not too much to pay to see Hayes's face.

CHAPTER XXIII

DAY OF RECKONING

THE BUSINESS TOOK longer than any of them expected.

Captain Blye gave them his available men, and the seal pelts were carried from the cave across the shoulder of hill to the beach. There the bundles were opened and inspected by Hayes. Many skins had been damaged with age and the incomplete curing. These had to be weeded out, the bundles made up again and freighted to the *Karluk* lying some distance out in safe anchorage. Everybody worked at it, even Marion, who kept tally of the pelts. Toward afternoon of the third day, since anchoring the *Karluk,* the anxiety was past. They knew that Hayes's fortune was assured—not fabulous riches, but, allowing for vagaries of the market price and usual accidents of carriage and trade, enough to let him repay Beach a good profit and leave himself comfortable.

A few pelts remained on the beach, enough for a last boat load. The boat would be coming soon for them. That would mark the end of their stay, the end of the chapter for Marion. After that there could be no more evading the issue. Jonathan Hayes had to be told the truth.

She had fallen back on the childish expedient of closing her eyes to the moment, of pretending the thing did not exist. Even now, sitting on a rock in the pallid sunlight she was thinking: "This thing isn't—not really! I'm not here, on a rock, somewhere in a wilderness. That glacier, the sea, the steamer, it's all a dream.

I'm really home, in the studio. Perhaps I ate Welsh rabbit last night—or is it too much smoking, I wonder!"

A step on the gravel behind her, a hand touching her shoulder gently, then Beach sat beside her on the rock. She thought Beach had gone back to the cave with Hayes. She didn't want to see Beach. She shrank from him uneasily.

Beach did not notice the shrinking. He was cheerful, had been cheerful, irritatingly cheerful these last days. He had paid no attention to her avoidance of him.

"Well, it's done. This is the last."

Marion made no answer, and Beach went on: "Yep. Glad of it, too. Somehow all this recent good luck—well, it's made me uneasy. Seemed too good to be true—after the other. I've jumped every time I heard a man cough. But we put it over. We sure did put it over! Are you glad, Marion?"

"Of course I am!"

"Yes. Yes, you ought to be. But you don't look it—"

"Stuff! I can't go round grinning all the time!"

"Hayes is glad, all right. The man looks ten years younger this afternoon. Ten? Twenty, I'll say. It certainly has been the making of him, poor old chap—"

"What do you mean, *poor old chap?*"

"Oh, nothing—I don't know! I like the fellow—and, of course, I feel rather sorry for him—about you, you know. Have you told him yet? Told him about us?"

She shook her head.

"Better do it. Really, you had better. And—Marion, you know I'm waiting for something—"

"Waiting for what?" Her voice sounded flat and strained.

"I've waited a long time for it, too long. It's this!" Beach caught her to him and kissed her. He kissed her savagely, hungrily, and she could not move in his close grasp. She had to submit. He began hurriedly, greatly shaken: "You're going to love me, Marion. You can't help but do it! If you knew how patiently I've waited, how I've had to fight to keep cool and play the game as you wanted it played! But that's over. Thank God it is over! We needn't pretend now."

At last he let her go, and she drew away. Her hand went to her lips, wiping them. It was as though his kiss had soiled her.

"No!" Beach was repeating. "We're done with show acting. What do you say we get married in Seattle—or for that matter, Blye! You know the captain of a ship can marry people!"

Marion gasped. Beach leaped at this new idea, plainly de-lighted with it. "Marion! Come on, are you game for that?"

She began to speak hurriedly, shakily, scarcely conscious at first of her intention. Fear of Beach—fear of his kisses, fear of a future with this man drove her to say it. "Beach! Listen to me, please. You've always been a good sport, Beach. You play fair, don't you? Yes! Everybody knows that. If I should say that I can't marry you—that I can never marry you, you'd believe me? Would you believe me?"

Beach stared. "No, I wouldn't. There isn't any reason in the world why you can't marry me. No reason—"

"There is! There's a reason—the best reason—"

"What reason?" Beach's face had passed from bewilderment to stubbornness that promised trouble. "What reason?" he de-manded in a tone that denied the reason before she gave it.

"Beach, I—I don't care for you—that way—can never care for you—that way. That's a reason, isn't it? Isn't that a good reason? Isn't it?"

"You don't mean that. You don't know what you're talking about. You do care—or you'll learn to care—"

"But I say I can't care. Not in a million years. Do you insist on it when I don't love you—can't ever love you?"

Beach rose from the rock and faced her, his gray eyes un-friendly, cold. "You're talking utter, damn rot," he said bluntly.

"I won't try to discuss love with you—or what you can do or can't do. I'm no heart-throb expert to advise silly girls—and I know very well you're not the kind of silly-girl that wants that advice. I do know that I care very passionately for you—and very tenderly. Marrying you means more than anything else to me. That's why I risked this trip—money, effort, dangers and all—because of you and your promise. We made a bargain. Now you're going to keep that bargain. Don't try to beg off!" Marion rose. "I made the bargain," she said with sad dignity. "I'll keep it—if you insist."

Beach's arms went about her shoulders.

"You do love me!" he cried. "You know you do. You'll find out—I'll teach you!" In vain she tried to avoid his lips, a sick loathing in her that made her knees tremble. His kiss gave her a frantic strength that thrust him back and left her gasping.

"Beach! That will do!"

Hayes had come down the hill and stood close beside them now, his look dangerous. Hayes's fists were doubled and he had difficulty keeping his tone even. "She doesn't like that, Beach. I wouldn't try it again if I were you."

Beach faced the Alaskan without giving a step. He was white and ready for blows.

"Suppose you keep out of this!" he said.

"I'll not keep out! I'll stay right here—"

"But if the lady asks you?"

"Asks me! Marion!" Hayes turned on the girl. She shrank from his look, seeming smaller, more frightened than ever.

"It's all right," Hayes said to her more gently. "Beach will apologize for annoying you—and it won't happen again."

Marion's lips opened to speak, but no sound came. She gestured helplessly.

"Marion," Beach said quietly, "I think we had better tell Mr. Hayes all about it. Shall I tell him?"

Marion exclaimed hurriedly: "No, no, please. I—I'll tell him!" In a moment more the two men would have been at each other's throats. Beach, she knew, was armed. And his look showed he would not stop short of killing. "Hayes—listen please. I—Beach and I—are going to be married—in Seattle."

Hayes made no sound or movement, but seemed to freeze as he stood.

"Yes, we're going to be married. I have promised," Marion said. She achieved a ghastly smile. "We're waiting for your congratulations, Hayes."

Hayes said thickly: "You promised to marry Beach? When?"

"Oh, some time ago. Several weeks ago, wasn't it Beach?" Her desperation gave her better composure. She had to act now, to pretend if she was to prevent tragedy. She pretended splendidly. "Yes, just before we left New York. But we thought we'd keep it quiet, you know. It's a fine thing for me, Hayes. I wish you'd appreciate that. *Mrs. Irving Beach!* Think of that! And we're going to have a regular house on Fifth Avenue, butlers and chauffeurs and a lot of big cars and—and everything! Maybe if you're very polite, you can come see us. My dear! If you knew the field I was running against. All the gals had an eye on Irving Beach, and I got him for my very own. For Heaven's sake, are you going to stand there like a wooden image or are you going to tell me you're glad for me—"

"Stop that chatter!" Hayes cried. "You say you're going to marry this man?"

"You heard me say it—"

"Why?"

"Just what do you mean by that? Why? Because I choose to, that's why—"

"Because you—love—him?"

"Love him? Of course I do!" Marion's indignation was superb. She went to Beach and her arms went about his neck. She looked up into his face and smiled fondly. "I'm marrying him because he's a dear, old sweetheart—and the girl isn't living that can resist him!" Deliberately she kissed Beach, clinging to him. From his arms she smiled at Hayes with every evidence of pride and happiness.

Beach, holding her fast, laughed briefly. "Well, Hayes, satisfied?"

"I see," Hayes murmured stupidly. "Yes—I see!" He started forward with an effort. "I'm very sorry—that I—misunderstood. You'll excuse my bad manners."

"Of course!" Beach extended his hand. "You must be friends!" Marion exclaimed. "I don't want you, boys, to quarrel like that again—ever! Wish me luck, Hayes!"

Hayes, towering above her, repeated gravely as if he had memorized a lesson: "I wish you both every possible good fortune—and happiness—together—"

Suddenly he turned his back on them. His stumbling movement told them the man was beaten down. All that was vital in him had been killed.

Hayes sat down on a rock at a little distance, his back toward them still. Her heart ached for him with a bitter, throbbing hurt—And then Beach clasped her and kissed her again. She bit her lips to keep back a scream.

But for all her effort she cried out at Beach's embrace—a sharp, broken cry of protest that roused Hayes.

What happened immediately, though, put all thought of the girl in the background for the time.

The boat from the *Karluk* was landing. A half dozen men were leaping out of it. All of them carried rifles. More astonishing still was the broad shouldered, sturdy, red-bearded man who led them all and greeted the astounded looks of the trio in the cove with a wide, thin-lipped grin. The man was Captain Darius Cook.

CHAPTER XXIV

THINGS MADE PLAIN

DARIUS COOK'S BEHAVIOR was almost as startling as his appearance in this lonely little cove of the bay of glaciers. On the three astounded onlookers he bestowed scarcely a glance at first. His mild voice broke into brisk orders.

"Two of you boys keep your guns on those folks. The rest of you pitch into those pelts and hustle 'em. That's the last of the lot, and we want to get out of here ahead of dark. Now, boys!"

The captain supervised the moving of the seal pelts, his back to the trio as if they did not exist at all. But two sailors with rifles kept them trained on Hayes and Beach and the girl, and though they, too, were grinning at the joke, they meant business.

Hayes found his voice first.

"Cook!" he shouted.

"My dear chap, in just a minute!" Cook glanced at them, and turned again to give final directions. Then he walked toward the three, walking deliberately, daintily, careful to avoid soiling his polished shoes. Cook was dapper as always, dressed in his neat blue serge, the customary silk shirt with a soft collar, the chaste and elegant tie, the gold sleeve links, a becoming soft hat covering his bald head. To Marion he removed the hat and made a little bow.

"Dear lady, we meet again—at last! Gracious, what a time it seems since that morning on Kalvik Island! But you're charming as ever. Youth is so splendid!"

"Look here," Beach said curtly, "what the devil does this mean?"

Cook grinned a little. "Mr. Irving Beach, of New York, I take it? We have never met, but of course I know you by reputation—"

"Just forget the play acting," Beach cut in. "Come down to cases. What are you doing here?"

"Why," Cook exclaimed, "didn't you know? Can't you guess? I am your fellow passenger—on the *Karluk*."

"It *was* he!" Marion gasped. "I did hear his voice that night!"

Cook looked slightly put out. "You heard my voice? On the *Karluk?* Dear me—I had no idea I had been so careless. Ah, I know now, the night you gentlemen called on Captain Blye— and almost surprised me. Of course. You managed to search the cabin quite cleverly, really! But, you see, I had slipped out. We had a panel cut through the wall just behind the captain's berth. It made a convenient door to my own little quarters, which, naturally, had to be kept a secret. Dear, dear, how nearly we came to being found out!"

Beach and Hayes exchanged startled glances. Cook's words made it plain that this plot had been well thought out and well carried out; that its beginning dated back to their own start.

"Good Lord!" Beach gasped. "How long has this thing been going on?"

Cook gloried in explanations. "Since you left New York, my dear fellow. Oh, yes, before that, even. You Easterners never seem to give us proper credit for intelligence, Beach. Why, I began my work as soon as you made it possible to take this trip. I had my backer as well as Hayes—a man fairly well known to both of you—ready to match dollar for dollar with you when it comes to getting these pelts—"

Marion interrupted with a cry: "That man is Douglas Fox! I know it!"

Cook bowed again. "A woman's intuition is almost uncanny," he applauded.

"You spied on us and tagged along, did you?" Beach burst out indignantly.

Cook laughed. "You might put it that way. And, Beach, as a business man, you must admit it was a shrewd stroke coming on the *Karluk*. Fox was ready to charter a ship, to go to any amount of trouble to follow you up and take the pelts away from you. But I, in my crude way, am a student of efficiency. I pointed out to him how unnecessary it was to go to the expense of two vessels when one was all that was needed. Our only real difficulty was in getting you to take the *Karluk*. It was there that the planning came in. Yes, and I must give credit to Al Sapley—"

"Sapley!" Hayes exclaimed.

"I told you that little rat would double-cross his own mother if there was a dollar in it for him," Marion said bitterly.

Hayes considered the revelation in stunned silence.

Cook went on. "Yes, Sapley did good work. He managed the cancellation of your first charter and kept you from getting that other boat in Seattle. By that time we had made all necessary arrangements on the *Karluk,* and my good friend Blye came to you with his splendid offer." Cook laughed silently. "If there are any other questions I'll be glad to answer them. I'm crude, I know. I lack the advantages of Mr. Beach with his wealth and business ability. But in my humble way I want you to understand I'm capable of taking a trick now and then."

The three prisoners were silent. Under Cook's genial manner they detected signs of a purpose that meant them no good. Cook was planning active deviltry and gloating over the revelation he was holding back.

Hayes burst out roughly: "You damn scoundrel! You dog! You mean to murder us. Murder—that's your plan!"

Cook rolled his eyes. "Hayes!" he expostulated. "My dear, good chap, you shock me!"

"Look here," Beach cried, "just what do you mean to do?

Let's hear the rest of your clever plans. We admit you did very well and very cleverly.

"Well?" Cook said mildly: "I mean to take the seal pelts, of course. I've wanted them these last couple of years, since I first heard of them. Now that they're safely aboard the *Karluk* at last, there isn't very much more to do, is there? We'll say good-by and get under way—"

"Leave us here?" Beach cried.

Cook shrugged. "I'm afraid I'll have to do that. What else can I do? Look at it from my point of view, Beach. It would be most embarrassing to take you along—in fact, I couldn't think of it."

"Murder us in cold blood, would you?"

"Oh, not murder—"

"You know it's murder," Hayes interrupted sternly. "It's murder as certainly as if you order these men to shoot us down. Murder and torture—the torture of slow starvation, cold, exposure. And you condemn a woman to that!"

"My dear Hayes! I've heard you boast you grew up among the Aleuts. Surely you can manage to live off the country. Eventually you ought to be able to find some settlement—though I'll admit that may take you several months."

"Listen to me," Hayes said. "I call this murder, and you know it is. I can live off the country, yes. These two can't. A frail woman—and this man, a man who's never been off a yacht or outside a millionaire's shooting camp. If you were a man you'd kill them in cold blood and be done with it."

Cook shrugged. "It's the best I can offer. No use arguing that."

Hayes seemed on the point of doing something desperate. His wild eye and twitching lip showed a man tried beyond human endurance. The armed men pressed forward their rifles apprehensively. But Hayes conquered himself by an effort, and grew calmer.

"Listen to me," said Hayes. "You can do better than that. I

sha'n't appeal for any mercy from you; there is no mercy in you. But I can show a plan much better—and much safer for you. I'm surprised at you, Cook! You're crude, after all! Clumsy! You mean to sail away from here with a cargo of pelts to which you have no title—stolen goods. Not only that—you propose to saddle yourself with the chances of apprehension for our murder! Do you call it clever to stack the cards against yourself that way?"

"I'm open to reason," Cook said curtly. "Show me a better plan."

"By right of discovery these pelts are mine," said Hayes. "Suppose I gave you a bill of sale for them? That would make them yours, and no questions asked when you sold them?"

Cook nodded. "That would clear up a minor difficulty. Go on."

"Give this man and woman safe passage to Kodiak Island. Give me your promise before these men of yours you will do this thing, and I will give you that title to every seal pelt in the lot. Is it a bargain?"

"And you?"

"I'll take my chances here. By myself."

Beach gasped. "You wouldn't do that!"

"I certainly will." Hayes spoke with cool confidence. "I'm not afraid to take that chance. I know the land—"

Marion turned on him suddenly, her hands on his arm. "But, Hayes! The sealskins—they're yours—you wouldn't give them up—"

"The sealskins! What a little thing to give up!"

"No. You must not give them up. A little thing? They mean your good name. Remember what depends on your producing them. And now that you've won, you sha'n't give that up. You sha'n't!"

Hayes smiled a little in spite of his desperate purpose. "It strikes me I haven't much to say about that—except to make it a little easier for Cook to get rid of them. And I shall give them up if I can make that bargain. Cook, how about it?"

Cook said finally: "If Beach and Miss Reade will sign a pledge to keep absolute silence about this business—"

"They'll sign that pledge," Hayes agreed.

But Marion cried out: "No, no, Hayes! Never to tell—never to defend your name when you're called a swindler and worse? When everybody will say you lied about your treasure!"

"You will sign that pledge," Hayes dictated sternly. "Let them say what they please. It's nothing to me—nothing. Do you think I mind losing that when I've lost—you? I'll give you all that—for a wedding present."

"It seems the only way, Marion," Beach seconded. "Hayes stands a chance here. You don't. I'm afraid I wouldn't be much help, either. And you can't go alone—with this fellow. Yes, we'll sign, Cook."

"Very well," Cook agreed. "On that consideration I'll give you both passage—not to Kodiak Island—I can't take any chances even with your promise—but to a safe port. Just as quickly as I can get the pelts sold you two can go about your own business. Please get into that boat. We must hurry."

Hayes wrote a bill of sale on a leaf of his notebook and gave it to Cook. Beach turned to Hayes and thrust out his hand, Hayes taking it silently. Half hysterically, Marion would have clung to the Alaskan. She was at a loss for words. Her eyes filled and she began to cry incoherently.

"Good-by," Hayes said gently. And then to Beach: "Take her. Don't waste time."

Beach led Marion to the boat. Cook and his men went with them, but the captain posted one man to make sure that Hayes did not stir.

The men shoved the boat afloat. All got in, and the oars were out. Hayes stood where they had left him, like a man of stone. His strong hands dangled lifeless at his sides. His head was bent and his gray eyes looked up from under heavy brows, looking his last on the woman he loved, who had taught him much and had raised high hopes only to smash them down.

Marion, staring back at him, had that scene burned indelibly in memory—the little cove strewn with boulders, the bit of beach, the black growth of forest behind, and the giant figure of a man who stood so still, so passive, giving up everything that she might go safely. Something within her was ready to break with grief, with protest at the horror of this sacrifice for her.

Cook's voice spoke suavely: "Good-by, dear old chap. Give my love to the Aleuts if you ever see them again."

Then that something in Marion's breast snapped. She sprang to her feet and had leaped from the boat before a hand could touch her.

She splashed through the shallow water and was running toward Hayes, crying passionately: "Hayes! Hayes! I won't leave you. I'll never leave you! I lied, Hayes! I love you—only you! I'll never leave you again!"

At Marion's words Hayes came to life with a start. He charged toward the boat. Whether he meant only to meet the girl, or meant to take vengeance on Cook, was not plain. But to Cook, his nerves already at the breaking point, ready to explode into a frenzy, it was plain Hayes meant mischief. Cook was on his feet, taking deliberate aim.

As Marion glanced over her shoulder she saw the captain's intention, and blocked his line of fire.

In the boat Beach and Cook grappled. The pistol cracked once, and Beach reeled back. Cook aimed again, a deliberate shot that found Beach's heart. The sportsman toppled out of the boat, half in the water, half on the sand, dead.

Marion ran up the sand. Cook turned from his murder, leaped ashore, and was after her, gun waving, when Hayes found his own weapon, and checked the crazed captain with a well-placed shot. Hayes dashed across the rocks, seized Marion in his arms, and dragged her hurriedly behind a big boulder. Crouching there, he turned his fire on the men in the boat.

CHAPTER XXV

AN OUNCE OF CAUTION

FOR A FEW minutes, while Hayes's scattering shots raked the beach and forced the men in the *Karluk's* boat to cower under the gunwale, the Alaskan ruled events in the cove. From behind the sheltering boulder Hayes could not see Cook. When the bullet caught him in the arm the captain spun on his heel and dropped. Hayes did not know whether he had killed or maimed his man. He hoped that he had killed him.

Besides Cook five men had come ashore from the *Karluk*. All had rifles. Hayes's first shots sent them to cover, and Cook's fall deprived them of leadership. One or two stray shots were sent after the Alaskan, but the men had no particular interest in the fight. Several were working with desperate caution to get the boat off the beach. A shout from Cook stopped that. Responding to his orders, the five left the boat and deployed, running in various directions for the cover of rocks and logs.

Hayes with one pistol could do no more than pump a few shots in their general locality in the hope of a lucky hit. Once these men were separated he knew very well his chances dwindled. They could come at him from six different ways if they chose, cut him off, kill him at leisure. And when they killed him, what of Marion? Answering the scattering fire, Hayes turned to study the land behind him. The boulder under which Marion and he lay was backed up against the shoulder of hill. The hill rose steeply, an earthen bank, slippery with mud and for a space of fifty feet without cover of even a shrub. But behind that lay the scrub timber. There was no other avenue of retreat; if they were to use this it must be done at once.

"There's just a bare chance to get out of this. Will you risk it?" he asked Marion.

Her eyes met his, unafraid. "I'll go where you go."

"Up that bank, then. It's slippery. They may get us. But take the pistol. If I'm hit you can use it—as you see fit."

"Cook won't touch me alive," the girl said soberly. Then for just a moment her face became piteous. "Hayes, I don't want to die! I love you!"

Hayes stooped swiftly and kissed her, briefly, passionately. "If it has to be, die fighting!" he whispered. "You're not afraid now!"

"No, I'm not afraid."

Hayes rose, and Marion followed him. They sprang at the slippery bank and began to climb, using hands and feet at the task.

For a moment they were not observed. Then the bullets began to *sput-sput* in the mud about them. With a shout five men were up from cover and after them. The exception was Cook. He stood still, taking more careful aim.

It was a nightmare task to climb that slippery bank. The bullets sang about them. Their feet found holes that crumbled and left them floundering. Marion, thus betrayed, was slipping back. Hayes reached down cautiously, grasped Marion's hand, and drew her up.

The five pursuers finally heeded Cook's orders. All stopped and began a deliberate fire. Several bullets went through the loose folds of Hayes's coat. Another seared the flesh of Marion's arm.

She looked up at Hayes and smiled. "We'll die—game—kid!"

The shooting had stopped. Hayes did not risk a second to find out why. In that lull he inched himself upward again, found firmer footing, and dragged the girl with him. They scrambled, then rolled over the top of the bank, and found themselves in the shelter of thick brush.

Lying flat, they crawled deeper into the cover. At last from behind a log they ventured to peer down into the cove. Cook and his men were standing still, as if under a spell. They heard then, having time to hear and understand sounds ignored before, the hoarse bellow of the *Karluk's* whistle.

The whistle was sounding short blasts: one, two, three, four—one, two, three, four. In the frantic repetition the voice of steam and brass took on a character. It was shouting like some living thing, and its call was a cry of alarm, of urgent appeal. As they looked the six listening men were galvanized to activity. They ran for the boat and got it awash. They pushed out, and the oars dipped, raggedly, hurriedly, each stroke conflicting with the other. They could hear Cook's screamed order for rhythm.

Hayes leaped up suddenly.

"I know!" he exclaimed. "I know what it is. Come here. Look!"

He dragged Marion, breathless, to a spur of the rock. They stood out on it, unafraid. From this vantage they could see down the channel to where the *Karluk* lay at anchor, spurts of steam rising from her whistle. And beyond, around the bend of the channel, came another vessel—a white-painted vessel with a sharp bow and buff stack, a smart, warlike, deadly efficient craft that ripped the quiet water of the *fjord*.

"The *Bear!*" Hayes shouted exultantly. "The revenue cutter *Bear*. They got my message!"

"Got your message?" Marion gasped. "What message?"

Hayes was smiling grimly, his dark eyes alight. "This is Cook's finish. He can't wriggle out now! I've got him."

"What is it? What have you done?" Marion was crying, shaking him frantically in her impatience.

"When we touched at Kodiak Island I sent word. I had the Indian woman take word across the island for me. I asked for the cutter—told them where to find us. It was just a wild guess—a precaution. Your fright on the *Karluk* that night prompted it. It kept me worrying, worrying for fear Cook might come—that he might fool us in some way. So I sent for the cutter. It's the ounce of precaution that saved us. Look—look at the men in that boat! They won't try for the *Karluk* now. They'll try to land—to get into the woods!"

From their height they could see the drama in detail.

The *Karluk's* boat had swung off its path toward the steamer. Now it was headed straight across the inlet toward the farther shore, its plain purpose to escape the revenue men.

Cook was steering. They could see his bald head plainly, even the peculiar, wounded awkwardness of his helpless left arm. He had swung the small boat in toward the glacier and was skirting the front of the ice ramparts.

"God!" Hayes gasped. "I believe they will make that shore! But I'd hate to be under that ice!"

Always the glacier was showering its fragments. Always there was the danger from some huge block splitting away and toppling into the sea. The man and woman on the rock, clinging tight to each other in their excitement, watched the small boat crawl along under the menacing palisade and forgot to breathe. The air about them shook with a sharp explosion. The cutter had fired a gun, directing a shot across the bows of the *Karluk's* boat, a signal to turn back.

Then the watchers saw something that killed their mutual cry of alarm before it was spoken, constricting their throats, depriving them of all volition. They could only watch, terrified.

When the echoing reverberation of the signal gun died they heard first the rattle of small ice blocks, the fall of loose trash along that half-mile rampart, dislodged by the concussion. But after that fall came the preliminary groan and crackle of fissures spreading like jagged lightning through a solid block of the glacier wall. The eye could actually see the darting lines of cleavage as they spread through the translucent green and blue that sparkled so prettily in the late sunshine.

Nature's mechanism worked with a deadly efficiency and precision that was awful to watch.

The men in the *Karluk's* boat had ample warning of their fate. They could be seen pulling frantic strokes to get their craft from under the breaking rampart. The horrified watchers on the rock saw the detail of it all, groaning aloud when one oar snapped under a madman's strain and the oarsman tumbled among his fellows.

The preliminary creaking and cracking of the ice burst into a great crescendo of sound, a terrifying, earth-shaking boom that stunned the ears.

A vast, ragged block of ice, fully fifty feet high and as thick through and wide, a towering berg, fairly leaped from the mother wall and loomed above the pigmy boat, rocking in an arc farther and farther off balance until it fell and all sign of man was blotted from the picture.

Of all that had happened in that last crowded hour there remained but one visible sign—the body of Beach sprawled on the sand of the cove.

The *Karluk* was bound south.

Captain Blye no longer commanded the steamer. The revenue department had assigned a competent young lieutenant to take her to Seattle and land Hayes and his treasure safely.

Blye had gone aboard the cutter *Bear,* a prisoner, to stand trial before a Federal commissioner. The captain had but one observation to make on the events of the voyage. As he was being taken off the *Karluk* he observed to Hayes with his usual economy of words: "Cook was a damn fool; so'm I."

Hayes and Marion watched him off in the cutter's small boat. His head was sunk, chin on chest. A soft felt hat was pulled over his eyes. His arms were folded. He looked the very picture of a second-rate Napoleon going to his Elba.

On a fine, clear night Hayes and Marion stood at the *Karluk's* stern, watching the eerie fairy fireworks of the aurora. Jagged spears of light, like the lances of a massed battery of searchlights, wheeled and clashed, climbing as high as the zenith and falling back again. Pulses of rose and violet and amber and green and blue throbbed and wavered.

The mysterious activity, its unceasing change and unfailing beauty, held them quiet a long time. Marion sighed finally: "And once I told you about the bright lights of Broadway! And I grinned to myself, thinking how they would awe you! Of all the unutterably silly, flatheaded ideas! Hayes, I'm just a plain, city fool!" Hayes's arm tightened about her. He said nothing, but the caress of that arm comforted and reassured her that he didn't agree in her self-valuation.

"When we've sold the pelts," Marion went on earnestly, "when everything is settled, and we're married—will you take me back to Kalvik, Hayes? Will you teach me your country—and the things that are worth knowing?"

"But, my dear, you'd die of loneliness away from Broadway!"

"Broadway! Hayes, I'd die of suffocation there. That cheap, sham stuff. That hokum! You've taught me things. I'm beginning to understand there is something better and bigger than that. Things that civilization stifles. Don't take me back there, ever! It's rotten!"

Hayes shook his head slowly. "No, just partly rotten—and lots of it sound. For you've taught me, too—you've made me want the best that civilization has to offer. The big thing, as I see it, is not to let the bright lights and glitter fool you about Broadway—or my own country. The real gold doesn't advertise—you have to look for that. So we won't give up your civilization altogether."

Marion came closer into his arms.

"Maybe you're right—maybe, some day, I'll find I'm homesick for that stuff, after all—"

"Then you shall have it. We'll try to get the best out of all of it."

She sighed contentedly. "Whatever you say goes, old dear!"

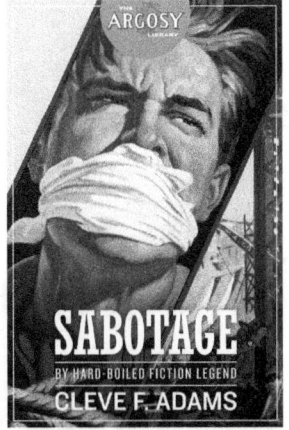

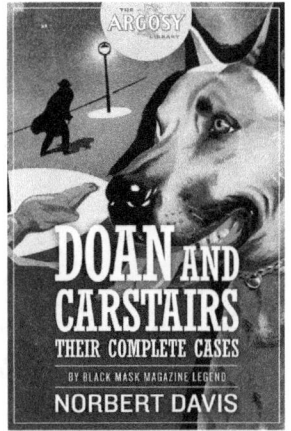

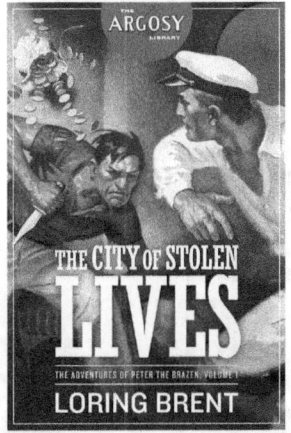

SERIES 2 • AVAILABLE SPRING 2015

THE ARGOSY LIBRARY™

SERIES 2 INCLUDES:

* BRAND * BRENT * ADAMS *
* MacISAAC * ROSCOE *
* GIESY & SMITH *
* BECHDOLDT *
* MONTGOMERY *
* FARLEY *
* DAVIS *

THE BEST FICTION
FROM THE FRANK
A. MUNSEY LINE

www.ingramcontent.com/pod-product-compliance
Lightning Source LLC
Chambersburg PA
CBHW071838020726
47502CB00004B/1414